The Salty Eleanor

by Matthew E. Nordin

Shadows of Eleanor

book three

This is a work of fiction. All of the characters, organizations, and events portrayed in his novel are either products of the author's imagination or are used fictitiously.

Cover art by Arden Ellen Nixon © 2020
www.ardenellennixon.com
www.patreon.com/ardenellennixon

The Salty Eleanor / Shadows of Eleanor, book 3
ISBN: 978-1-7355573-0-4

For the coffee shop owners who allow authors to linger.

1

"Did you lace this brew with troll's blood?" Sindrick coughed as he slid the mug away. The frothy liquid sloshed onto the table. "It's supposed to make you forget one night, not tomorrow's as well. Dan's bride will have strong words with you if it does."

Dan eyed the brew carefully as Sindrick motioned for him to drink.

Although they were the same height, Sindrick's muscles were more defined. Most of them were gained by swinging a hammer at the blacksmith's forge. He would be there tonight if it weren't for the special event.

"It's not that strong," Jack said from behind them and slapped Sindrick on the back. He was the shortest of the apprentices but the biggest boaster. "You need to toughen your gut." He grabbed the cup, tapped it on the others, and threw back a swig into his gullet. "Oh sweet heaven's fire! You might be right." His face turned red as he placed both hands on the table.

"It's got meat to it," Sindrick warned Dan, who picked a mug up and held it tentatively to his lips. "Go on and pay your dues. If Jack would divulge the secrets of his master's brew, I could improve it for you."

"If you show me how to make those fancy stone mugs, I might consider it," Jack said and pointed to the empty vessel in front of him. "They're light as wood and nearly unbreakable. You probably owe me for the family secrets I gave you to use with your alchemy. Just don't start selling any drinks to the barkeep. This place already has the best supply from me."

"If you say so." Sindrick had to admit the mixing of metals fascinated him more than whatever potion Jack's family brewed. "There's hardly a swallow left for you, Dan. Go on and take a step closer to your maker."

Dan's eye twitched as he sipped the drink. "I'm glad there's a hint of honey. Makes the bitters a little more bearable."

"Given the drinks he creates, Jack should have all the women in town swooning over him," Sindrick said and nudged the brewer's apprentice. "I'm surprised Dan's getting shackled up before you and Kate do. How long have you courted her?"

"We're good where we're at, and it keeps things simple." Jack stood up. "Besides, I don't see anyone flocking to you with your ugly mug." He playfully jabbed Sindrick in the arm.

"I'm happy to be settling down," Dan chimed in. "Rena is perfect for me. I want to raise a family and teach my kids how to weave and spin yarn. It took me all week to get our garments ready for the wedding. A few extra hands to help will be nice."

"You'll be a right taskmaster." Jack laughed. "I'm surprised you didn't have us do the work with it being your last night as a free man. Traditionally, you're supposed to be taking things lightly."

"Ah, it's not a bother. Each should strive to better what they've been gifted. You stick to improving these drinks." Dan finished the last of the brew and set the mug back on the table. "Okay, it does taste like a fairy puked into it, but it's better than a troll's blood brew as Sindrick aptly named. Don't get any ideas for your next concoction."

Jack winked at him and ran back to the barkeep, ordering another round of drinks.

"Speaking of trolls," Sindrick said while he gathered his hair behind him and started to braid it back. "Has anyone seen Crowell, yet? He should've been ready with the groom's midnight voyage."

"He's probably mapping out a path to find the troll island and have us raze the place." Dan shook his head. "He's obsessed with them."

Sindrick had to shove his chair back as Jack stumbled over it to get their drinks on the table.

The stone mugs had been one of the most popular items at the tavern. Through the referrals, Sindrick gained a small stream of income—one he hoped would eventually become large enough to afford his own forge. Both of his friends were already set to leave their apprenticeships.

"I heard Crowell once outran Gostav, the great king of the trolls." Jack swirled his drink around before chugging it down. "The blighter probably didn't see our good captain and was traveling in the opposite direction."

"I did outrun the troll king," a deep voice boomed behind them. "Gostav was lucky I wasn't armed."

The man walking up to the table towered over the other three. His sleeveless shirt was tight to enhance the size of his biceps, larger than the size of Sindrick's leg. There was a reason the other apprentices called him captain. Although he was their equal, no one liked to question his decisions.

"Also, you shouldn't drink anything Jack made tonight," Crowell continued and placed his behemoth hands on the table. "I've smuggled in some of the strongest ales you'll ever taste. Made a good deal with a farmer in Raikrune."

"I've heard rumors of those lands," Jack said and raised an eyebrow. "They say the magic there has been lost. I think it's a bunch of wealthy people feeding off the fear of the poor. Nothing but whispers of ancient spells and ghost towns."

"To those who don't know where to look, it may seem like illusions." The tavern chair creaked under Crowell's weight as he sat on the other side of the table. He lifted one of the drinks and sniffed it.

"You should dive for the bottom on that stuff," Dan said. "It'll put hair on your hairs."

A crack of thunder shook the room before Crowell could respond.

"So much for going on a voyage tonight." Sindrick looked out the window and sighed. "We can find somewhere else to celebrate. The forge is always heated."

"Nonsense." Crowell stood up boldly and jammed his thumb into his chest. "They don't call my ship the Stormeye for nothing. It's a good night for hunting spirits on the seas. We'll get Dan a proper send off to his life of captivity."

He punched Dan's arm so hard, the tailor almost fell out of his chair. The drink in front of Sindrick didn't fare so well. It spewed its contents onto his pants.

"Watch it!" Sindrick moved his chair back from the stream of liquid running off the table. "We don't want to ruin Dan's handiwork. He probably spent more time working on his wedding trousers than he did planning for the ceremony."

Dan's mug hit Sindrick in the shoulder. It spilled more of the rank drink onto his shirt. He stood up as Dan burst into a fit of laughter.

"Now you look like a fairy puked on you," he said between breaths.

Another clap of thunder and flash of lightning filled the room. The pattering of rain on the roof added to the noise as more patrons entered the tavern to escape the storm.

"I guess I'm already soaked," Sindrick said. "Might as well get rinsed off in the rain. Lead the way, captain."

Crowell nodded and gulped down the last remaining drink. The others followed him out of the warmth of the building and into the harsh night.

Sindrick was likely the soberest of the group and hoped to remain that way. None of his friends would be able to remember the night, which meant he could retell the story however he wanted.

Yet, no drink could cause Sindrick to forget that singular moment of merriment. It would be the last time all four of them remained in such good spirits with one another.

The roar of the waves beating against the ship added to the adrenaline coursing through Sindrick's veins. He'd been on many trips with Crowell, who liked to recount his stories of sailing through tremulous waters and weather. However, the captain was known for his embellishments, and this was the worst Sindrick experienced.

Crowell had pushed the ship out to sea as if it were a calm, sunny day. The strength of Jack's drink he guzzled likely helped with his boldness to depart.

"Are you sure the boat can handle these waves?" Dan called out from his binds. As was tradition, he had been tied to the mast before the four departed. "I'd like to have a wedding night tomorrow."

Crowell flashed his teeth into a smile and spun the wheel quickly to cut through a wave about to curl over them.

"I wouldn't worry about our captain," Sindrick said, steadying himself on an overhanging rope. "He knows what he's doing. The seas would be mad to try to stop him." He gripped the rigging tighter, knowing his words were meant to convince himself as well. "You should be thankful you're secure. Jack looks like he's about to fly out."

Sindrick pointed to their smaller friend, who was clutching onto the side rail. His face showed a green tint, and he struggled to keep his balance. Every so often, he would stick his head over the edge.

"He can't handle his own drink." Dan laughed. "Bring me another swig Crowell's stash. He definitely found something good. I need to remember to get some for the ceremony."

"Too much of it, and you'll likely marry everyone you meet." Sindrick grabbed a bottle and tipped it to Dan's lips.

Dan strained to get a drink while being bound and tossed from the storm. Most of the liquid spilled across his chin.

"Easy with my bottles!" Crowell shouted from behind the wheel. "It's not like the cheap stuff Jack makes."

"It's for Dan anyway," Sindrick said and took a deep drink of it. The smooth taste of caramel and pineapple danced on his tongue. The liquid slid down his throat. "This is a dangerous drink. I could probably down a whole keg of this before getting sick."

"With how desperate you are to find someone, I'd advise against it," Crowell said and gave him a wink.

Sindrick coughed from the remark. "How did you get that idea? I don't remember saying anything about it," he said more to himself.

"You'd be a fool not to think about it at your age." Crowell held up his hand to shield his eyes from the salty spray of the waves. The storm gave them a break from the torrential rain. "We're almost out of it."

"Jack will be happy to hear that." Sindrick offered more of the bottle to Dan, who pursed his lips out to get every drop. "It seems like these storms blow through fast this time of year. I'm glad it's a warm rain."

Dan coughed. "How long am I supposed to stay tied up? It's not for the whole time, is it?"

"You know you can't be untied until we stop," Crowell said and kicked one of the levers on his boat. "We'll set you free in a moment. Once we get through this clearing, I want to show you all something I discovered on my last trip."

Crowell turned the ship again into the complete darkness of the storm's fury. The last wall of rain fell on them as they passed through a low hanging cloud. Although the waves remained high, it was a relief to be out of the wind.

"Hey Jack, the storm's gone," Crowell called. "Get over here and join us. You can undo the knots around Dan while you're at it. Sindrick doesn't know how to untie a vest."

Sindrick waved him off and looked out across the sea.

The clear break in the sky showed him an endless amount of stars filling every inch of space. Each one shone brighter than the next, creating the dazzling map of the night. It gave him an overwhelming sense of loneliness.

He didn't want to admit his deep longing to find a woman worth settling down with, but his companionship was becoming scarce. Dan would be married by tomorrow, and Crowell was always off seeking new adventures. Jack was practically living with Kate, and it wouldn't be long before they would be married too.

Sindrick wanted to say he had a prospect, but none of the girls he liked in Virfell stayed long. No one wanted to live in the town for good if they could leave. The lackluster trade market remained dismal, and the terrible winters scared off any travelers from settling.

"Gentlemen, please entertain my words," Crowell said ceremoniously and descended onto the deck as Jack freed Dan from his ropes. "I know most of you view sailing as a poor man's craft, and I could never have as much prestige or honor as your noble pursuits. I can't craft a drink to alter your thoughts or fashion an indestructible mug. Even Dan has me beat with his ability to weave yarn into something useful."

"It impressed one fine lady." Dan smiled. "And that's all I care about."

"I don't know if I could settle on one," Crowell continued and grabbed the bottle from Sindrick. He lifted it to his lips, looking off into the distance before taking a swig. "But one thing I've been after is the knowledge of forgotten times. The places I've recently visited uncovered some things you could not fathom."

"Not to mention all the diseases you likely picked up," Jack said with a grin. His color had returned with his wit. "Come on, great captain. What sort of devilish tricks have you been learning?"

"Sindrick likely knows more than me about what can be hidden beyond our vision." Crowell handed the bottle back and rubbed his hands together. "You've told me how an ordinary stone or gem could have hidden properties, am I right?"

"Yes." Sindrick nodded. "Almost every material has a special quality waiting to be unlocked. My father dabbled in the mysteries of alchemy and showed me how a blacksmith could use the true abilities of a metal."

"Well, I've learned about the magic of the sea." Crowell stepped to the center of his ship. "This will be something you won't see again, so I hope you enjoy it, Dan."

He began to mutter in an unknown language. His tone dropped to a lower pitch as he called for an entity from the deep to be revealed. He placed his hands upon the deck and shouted in the strange tongue.

The water around them churned, more so than in the storm. It rippled in odd shapes like rain fell from underneath the waves.

"Best find your spot at the rail." Dan nudged Jack. "Looks like the captain is bringing something down on us."

"Not down," Sindrick peered over the edge and wiped the water from his eyes. "Something is coming up!"

The patterns of the waves increased in their vibrations and intricacy. They pulsed away from the ship.

Sindrick leaned closer to the water. They weren't waves, they were wings.

"What have you—" He gasped as the waves exploded into a flurry of small birds, flying upside down.

The birds rose into the air and spun around the ship, transparent like the water dripping off them. Each one remained the same distance from the one in front of them. They continued to create a pillar of tiny diamond shapes, floating higher around the ship.

"This is incredible." Dan was wide-eyed and held a hand out to touch them.

"Stop!" Crowell yelled and reached for Dan's arm. He was too late.

Dan barely grazed one of the birds, and he quickly fell back in shock.

His finger started to smoke and blister. He screamed in pain while the others watched the skin and bone curl back. No blood spilled out from the severed finger as it fell off and cauterized itself.

"Call it off!" Sindrick grabbed Crowell's shoulder and spun him around. "Whatever this is. End it."

Crowell looked too terrified to respond. His mouth hung open.

"You could have warned us not to touch them," Jack said and shoved him back to bandage Dan's hand.

"I didn't know." Crowell stared up at the increasing multitude of creatures swarming around the ship. "They never stayed this long. It's a simple spell that was supposed to be done in seconds. I don't know how to stop them."

Everyone huddled closer together and held their breath for what seemed like an endless nightmare.

The birds continued to circle in their upside-down formation higher into the night. Their haunted shrieks echoed with the chaotic waves. They finally vanished into the sky, and the seas became still again as if nothing had occurred.

"We need to get back to town and find a healer." Sindrick put a hand on Dan's back. "Are you okay?"

"I think so," Dan said. "I've never felt so much pain. It kept getting worse until the birds left." He looked down at his hand. "My finger?"

"At least it wasn't the one for your wedding band," Jack said. "Rena would have the captain's head if it were."

"She's not going to be happy with you either way," Sindrick said to Crowell. "You may want to rethink your plans of attending the ceremony tomorrow."

Crowell didn't appear to be listening. He continued to be transfixed on the place where the creatures disappeared.

"Give me more rum," Dan said through clenched teeth. "This night can't get any worse."

They continued to drink more in an attempt to forget the strange events they had witnessed, but there was not a strong enough brew. An evil presence seemed to follow them back to Virfell as Crowell silently guided his ship to harbor.

2

Heat from the forge caused sweat to run into Sindrick's eyes as he worked feverishly to keep his mind away from the previous night's events. The lingering effect of the strong drinks didn't help the dehydration headache, pounding in his head. He needed to replenish his thirst and set the hammer aside.

A jar of water near the door remained fresh in the early morning, chilled from the Virfell air that became cooler during the autumn. Although the season was not as harsh as the hill country farther north, their winds blew down from icy peaks and made everyone wish for a job by the forge.

"I thought you were going to take the day off," Sindrick's master said, nearly knocking the door into him as he entered. "How long have you had the forge running?"

The Salty Eleanor

"I set up early." Sindrick drank as much water as the ladle would hold and walked back to his anvil. "Everyone in the tavern admires my stone mugs. The brewer's apprentice commented on its sturdy form. It gave me inspiration for a new idea. Metal weaving helps with the durability, but I could craft an additional property to sustain its contents, whether it be hot or cold."

The master blacksmith rubbed his temple and gave a familiar look of impatience. "While your enthusiasm is admirable, we are getting behind on orders. I was out most of the morning doing deliveries and apologizing."

"I'm sorry, Malek. I came in early to work on orders, and I was going to get caught up. . . once I figured out the right blend of materials for the cup. It would be easier if I had more time to test my ideas."

Malek sighed and tightened a leather strap around one of his hammers. "When you can finish what I've tasked you to do on time, then you can delve into the alchemy projects that aren't profitable work. Some metals are not meant to be mixed, and there is much you have to learn about using effective combinations. I know you want to study more on your own, but the business must come first."

"But that is the best part about being a worker of the forge. Each material can produce different properties once it reveals a pattern to me. You have to feel the heart of the earth, understand the metal."

"It also wastes valuable time," Malek said and examined the iron rod at Sindrick's workbench. He inserted it into the glowing furnace and spoke softer. "Before your father left, he told me to teach you everything I learned from him. Many of his techniques I didn't understand. I believe that you will discover them one day—you've already found ways to enchant metals I never could. But right now, we need to finish these orders. And I must warn you, everything that enhances something must take it from somewhere else."

"So if I created an enchanted item, would a cursed one form in its place?" Sindrick asked and pulled the heated iron from the fire.

He jabbed the molten metal into a small pile of gems in front of him. The ruby hissed against the harder rock. With the right combination, they would create a new pattern of properties for Sindrick to study. He needed to reheat and shape it into a cup once the transfer of energy was complete.

"An ill-made item could draw its power right out of the creator," Malek said and refilled the jar of water. "It's happened before."

"You listened to my father's tales too much." Sindrick waved him off and returned to his crafting. "He always said my mother had been cursed, but the disease overtook her senses. Most people get sick here. It's the way of life in our lands. We have to get stronger so we can beat any—"

A strap of leather whipped Sindrick's back. He gritted his teeth from the shock and turned around sharply.

Malek wrapped the strip around his hand. "Do not speak of your father in such ways. He was the greatest smith in these lands. If he convinced himself of something to be true, it was true."

Sindrick shrugged. He wished his father told the truth. He wanted to believe his mother had somehow not gone mad with all the theories of curses and magic in metal. There was no magic, only the measurement of mixing the stone. The stones told their properties, and one had to read them correctly to make the enhancement.

"I'll trust these gems," Sindrick said and held up the clump of metal with the fused rubies. "They do not change unless I instruct them to. They don't leave when they become weak."

"You have much to learn." Malek sighed. "Your father should have been the one teaching you this. Work needs to come first before experimenting, understand?"

Sindrick nodded in agreement, but his passion for crafting could not be hammered away.

"Get the orders done for the plows." Malek pointed to a box of halfway sharpened metal. "We can talk about you having your own forge later, when you're not so bitter about your friends getting married."

"I'm not bitter," Sindrick replied too quickly. He had to admit that most of the others around his age had found someone to marry or moved away to find someone. "I might be fighting back the effects of what we drank last night. Jack's brews need a bit more flavor, but they do the trick."

He examined the staff with the rubies affixed to it. The way the metal mixed with the red gems showed its desired form. It did not want to be shaped into a cup. It wanted to draw blood—an indestructible sword with a desire to cut flesh.

Sindrick set it to the side.

"Swords after plows," he reminded himself.

The Salty Eleanor

The shop remained warm after the sun crossed to the far side of the building, and the glow from the forge provided enough light for Sindrick to continue working with his alchemical pursuits. He had finished the plows and stared at the rubied bar, ready to be shaped into a sword. Although Crowell was more of a bare-knuckle fighter, it would make an excellent gift for him.

Sparks danced across the blade as Sindrick pounded it flat with his hammer, melding the gem and metal properties together. He had to be precise. Too heavy of a hand, and he would beat out the abilities he'd observed. Patient strikes would prevail over rushed work.

"What are you still doing here?" a voice called from the other room. Malek stepped out. "Don't you have a wedding you're supposed to go to tonight?"

"How long has it been dark?" Sindrick almost dropped his hammer when he looked out the window.

"The sun went down a short while ago. When is the ceremony?"

"It started at sunset, but I should be able to make most of it," Sindrick said and left the half-forged sword on the anvil.

He ran over to furnace and stopped the wheel that spun air into the forge. His blackened hands smeared more residue onto his well-used apron while he tried to look more presentable.

"Use this," Malek said, returning with a bucket and clean garments. The dark brown shirt would hide any remaining grime.

Sindrick dunked his hands in the water and rubbed the hammerscale from around his eyes and cheeks. The shirt hung loosely over him, covering his black wrap pants. He grabbed a long vest of fur and tied it around his chest. The rest of his soot-covered belongings would be safe at the forge.

"I know I usually don't leave such a mess," he called to Malek, who gave him a look of disapproval. "I'll clean everything in the morning,"

"I'll allow you to spare the forge for your friends this time. If I didn't force you to leave, you'd likely work all night." Malek laughed as Sindrick rushed out the door.

"What did I miss?" Sindrick whispered to Jack, who was trying to blend in with the back of the crowd.

"It's about time you got here," Jack said and put an arm around him, bending low. His breath reeked of alcohol. "I'm joking with you. I was a tiny bit late too. The stuff I've got for

22

tonight is sweeter than anything you've ever had in your life. It'll make you wish it were legal to marry a drink."

"Have they done the fire show already?" Sindrick shrugged Jack's arm off him. "I heard some of them might be elven-kind."

"Why would an elf come here? I thought they hated us. Anyway, Dan's been tied to Rena, and the chief is about to give the final blessing."

"Good. I didn't miss it."

Jack hiccuped loudly while a few of the people gave them nasty stares. He placed a finger to Sindrick's lips. "We need to be quieter. You're too loud."

Sindrick leaned in closer to listen to the chief's words, but the crowd became excited. It would soon be time for the celebration of two souls igniting as one, Sindrick's favorite tradition.

The fire show symbolized the passion of marriage and gave the flame lighters a chance to show off their skills. Their normal routine was to secure the village's perimeter every night to keep any wandering beast or marauder at bay. At weddings, they got the rare opportunity to display their talents, enlisting others from distant lands to perform.

The entertainers circled the entire audience and twisted balls of fire in the air.

"You know, for being a poor tailor, Dan's going to be living on the pig's back with the wife he's found," Jack continued without regard to the volume of his voice. "She knows a lot about port cities and trading. Her family has deep pockets because of it."

"I'm sure we would all be better off if we left Virfell more often," Sindrick whispered and tried to pull his friend aside to avoid any more glares. "There's never anything new here. I've already experimented with every different combination of elements nearby." He watched the fire performers as Jack opened another bottle he'd smuggled under his coat. "The forge is so busy though. I'm not sure I'll ever get a chance to leave."

"You'll find your path. I'm sure of it." Jack handed his drink to Sindrick. "Kate is always trying to convince me to move east. You can slap me if I'm wrong, but I think these twirlers came from there. No one born here has those types of skills."

The jugglers flipped blazing ropes between their legs and around their necks. Each came dangerously close to singeing the skin of their fellow performers. One stood near the newlyweds and spun a hoop of fire around her waist. She kept it up with her hips, and it never touched the ground.

"I wonder if I could make something to burn brighter for them." Sindrick took a quick drink and thumbed through his pocket of gems. Whenever he was away from the forge, he liked to keep a small collection close in case any inspiration came to him. "I may have discovered something which can create a flame when two rocks are struck together."

"Yeah, it's called flint." Jack broke into a fit of laughter at his own joke.

"Not quite so primitive," Sindrick said. "It would last longer than normal kindling, and it would give more light."

"Excuse me," someone said beside them and put his hand on Sindrick's arm. "I overheard you speaking of elves and fire."

The stranger kept his head down to hide his face in a large hood. His other garments were a similar fabric to the fire jugglers' clothes.

"I know of trade opportunities between the elves and humans again," the figure continued and let the light reflect off a free strand of his auburn hair. "If you do discover something, I'd be interested. Although the elves prefer natural magic, our queen is quite fond of spells concerning fire."

"Your queen?" Sindrick asked.

The stranger winked and turned to the center of the crowd. He held his hand out to stop the other performers, removing his hood. Although mostly covered by a headband, Sindrick could see the elongated ears of an elf.

The jugglers ceased their twirling and let their fires die down, giving attention to the elven guest. He took a stick with a long flame on the end and held it above his head. Sparks flew into the evening sky as he flicked it with his finger. In a grand flourish, he flipped it around and placed the fire inside his mouth.

The crowd gasped at the spectacle, then cheered as he pulled out the extinguished stick.

"Are you going to stay for the party?" Jack asked after the elf bowed and the clapping subsided.

"I wouldn't miss it, especially with the company we have. Did you see what I saw?"

Jack shrugged. "I think so. But there's a hidden strength in this brew. I might be seeing fae soon."

Sindrick took the last drinks of the bottle's sweet contents. He turned it over carefully and peeked into it. "If you have more of this strawberry mead, I'll gladly escort you to the tavern."

"I'm surprised I could appease your eloquent taste," Jack said sarcastically. "I saved the good stuff for today. My experimental mixtures were for last night."

Sindrick laughed. "I have a bad feeling in my gut about what happened, but it wasn't because of the drinks." He pointed to Dan's hand which was tied to his wife's. The white bandage stuck out in contrast to the golden rope. "I'd hate to be there when he had to explain what happened. By the way, have you seen Crowell?"

"He showed up at the beginning and left as soon as they were tied. He's likely summoning something else dark and disastrous from the sea. I was told to watch out for that sort of magic. It brings more harm to the caster than the victim."

"I find it interesting, but I agree with avoiding it." Sindrick handed the bottle back to Jack and watched the performers finish the show with an enormous fireball. "It looks like they're almost done. Is Kate going to be at the celebration?"

"Oh, Kate." Jack looked across the crowd. "I was supposed to find her once the performance started. You distracted me."

"Hey, don't blame me for forgetting your true love."

"I'll tell her we were discussing something important." He put his hand on Sindrick's shoulder to boost himself higher as he searched. "If you see her first, say we were going over the speech you're giving tonight for Dan."

"What?" Sindrick coughed. "I didn't know we were giving speeches."

"That's what you get for showing up late." Jack punched him in the arm and ducked into the crowd to find Kate.

Sindrick rubbed his arm more out of shock than pain. Using the hammer all day made it numb.

"Are you local to this place?" a soft voice asked behind him. He turned to see a young lady staring at him intently. "I saw you speaking with one of the performers. Do you know the groom?"

"Yes," Sindrick said with a smile. The maiden seemed a little younger than himself but not part of their community. "Are you related to Rena?"

The girl laughed and shook her head. She looked around the crowd and frowned.

"You don't happen to know where they are celebrating after this, do you?" she asked and twirled a strand of her hair playfully between her fingers.

"It's going to be at the tavern." Sindrick's pulse raced.

The girl before him wasn't particularly the type he enjoyed the company of, but on second thought, he didn't have many options. The local girls he liked never returned the sentiment. It had been more seasons than he wanted to admit since he had courted anyone.

"Would you like to go with me?" he managed to sputter.

"We'll find our way there." She waved toward one of the fire jugglers who had finished his performance. He smiled at her and rushed to her side. "We may be a little late. Thanks for the help, sir."

Sindrick nodded and sighed while the two ran off into the night together.

He looked across the audience. Everyone he saw held hands with someone else while they strolled to the tavern. Some had the same look in their eyes as the girl and fire performer, who snuck away to share their passion.

Sindrick tried to stop the bitterness from creeping inside of him. Working solo helped him focus on what needed to be done, and the best company to keep was his own. However, he couldn't deny the longing for a wife weighed heavy on his soul.

3

The familiar pub was packed with high spirits and laughter. All manner of travelers and freeloaders mingled with the wedding attendees.

Sindrick decided to stick with the watered-down grog the bartender was serving to those not in the couple's immediate family. Jack had promised to save him a few pints of his special mead, but he hoped to keep his senses a while longer. There wasn't anyone he wanted to impress anyway.

Jack and Kate were already sitting with the newly married couple, surrounded by their families. The musicians played over the noise of the crowd, reassuring Sindrick that he wouldn't have to come up with a speech for Dan. Part of him wished he could rally the crowd in humor over their many exploits together. Dan was often too eager to do whatever the group suggested, at his own expense.

Sindrick turned back to his drink and blew across the surface of the liquid. The rippling of tiny waves made him wish to be out on the sea, searching for exotic lands and discovering rare elements for his alchemy.

He lifted the cup to his lips and closed his eyes to drink down the possibilities awaiting him outside the confines of the town.

It spilled down his shirt from someone ramming into his back.

"I'm sorry," a melodic voice whispered in his ear. "There are too many people in here."

"I've had worse," Sindrick said and almost dropped his cup when he turned around.

Before him stood a young woman who encompassed his vision of beauty. Her eyes swirled like the clear sky at night and mesmerized his while she raised an eyebrow. A dark green dress clung tightly to her body with a black corset in front, threaded delicately. The fur of her cape hanging over her shoulders appeared to be in pristine condition, never touched by foul weather.

"You are new here." Sindrick's words stumbled out. "I mean, I haven't seen you around here before. Do you live in Virfell?"

"You don't remember, do you?" Her lips curved up into a smile that highlighted the gleam in her eyes and made her look more mysterious. "I guess you can say I've returned after being gone a while."

"Oh, is your family local?" He moved over so she could slide next to him at the bar.

"We moved." She raised a finger to the barkeep, and he sat a glass of wine in front of her. The woman swirled its contents and returned her gaze to Sindrick. "It's funny coming back. So many people and places have changed and yet. . . you look about the same."

"What do you mean? How long ago did you move?"

"We were quite young." She drank the wine in one swallow and wiped off the drip sliding down her chin. "I remember you constantly asking your father if you could go with him to his forge. He always said no."

Sindrick looked down into his glass. He longed for one last opportunity to see his father working again, before he departed into the frozen lands without a goodbye.

"Sorry," the woman said. "I didn't mean to hit a soft spot. I always respected him, your whole family. Honestly, I had wished for us to be together someday, the fleeting hopes of youth."

32

She placed both hands on the bar and leaned forward to get the barkeep's attention again. He never turned to see her. She sunk back to her stool.

"So, what brings you back to Virfell?" Sindrick offered her some of his drink, but she wrinkled her nose and shook her head.

"I have my reasons." She looked around to see if anyone noticed the abandoned drink beside her. She put a finger to her lips and grabbed it. "You probably like me more mysterious, anyway."

"I can't argue with you there." Sindrick smiled as she held up the stolen drink.

Although he could not recall who this woman was, he was glad she remembered him. The way she threw back the second glass made him pause. She had to be coming from a harsh place, drinking to forget about it or celebrating her escape.

"You forgot to ask," she said slyly. "And I like to keep you guessing."

"What am I guessing?" Sindrick asked.

"My name." She rested her head in her hands and leaned on the bar. "You have no idea which family I was part of, do you? Your face gives away your obliviousness. It's cute."

"Thanks." Sindrick raised his glass. "Well, here's to the reuniting of old friends. I hope we can be again."

"If you ever find out my name, perhaps we could be more."

She quickly grabbed another glass and clinked it to his. He almost choked from the look she gave him. His cheeks grew flush.

"There you are," Jack said, interrupting them and grabbing Sindrick's shoulder. "You'd better get outside fast. Someone said Crowell is back, and Dan said he would wring his neck if he saw him again after what happened."

"That explains why he wasn't at the wedding for long." Sindrick turned to the woman. "Forgive me for not introducing my friend. This is Jack."

Jack held out his hand. "Pleased to meet you—"

"Eleanor." She shook Jack's hand and winked at Sindrick. "I'm sure the pleasure will be all mine. I'll let you two be about whatever it is you need to do. Don't keep me waiting too long, Sindrick."

"I'll go talk to Crowell." Sindrick sighed and pointed to Jack. "Keep Dan distracted with your special brew."

"It'll be no trouble whatsoever." Jack patted his cloak, which hid the strawberry mixture. "He's already six feet deep inside his

34

drink, and I've yet to introduce the good stuff. I'll make sure he's well lubricated."

"What would I need to do to sample some of this brew?" Eleanor asked him with a grin and turned to Sindrick. "If you want a taste of the good stuff, you'd better hurry back to me."

Sindrick's heartbeat pounded in his ears, and he cleared his throat. "For you, I don't want to miss a breath. I'll be quick."

He slipped out from the commotion of the tavern and into the cold night air.

His ears rang from the contrast of the noise inside to the silence of the town. Here, it was quiet. The darkness held its celestial breath in anticipation of the morning.

"Crowell?" Sindrick's voice echoed down the street. "Captain, are you out here?"

No one stirred. The great pine trees muted the sound of the wind blowing through them. The snow would blow in soon. He could smell the ice forming in the air, freezing all around.

"I missed you at the wedding," he called again. "Sorry. Do you need to talk?"

Sindrick strained his ears for a response. Nothing.

He rubbed his hands together and looked back to the tavern.

"Where did I meet Eleanor?" he asked himself.

She had a familiarity about her, but her presence felt new and exciting. It was as if his whole childhood had been a dream, and he couldn't remember the details. He hadn't slept well since his mother's death. The lack of sleep caused him to dream more during the day and forget past events. Yet, Eleanor's beauty went beyond anyone he could remember or imagine.

Sindrick sighed one last time to the glowing moon and headed back into the tavern. The light coming from the hearth and mass of bodies caused him to blink rapidly.

"What are you doing here?" Dan's angry voice raised above the others in the crowd.

Sindrick stumbled back in alarm, thinking it was about him until he followed Dan's gaze to a spot at the bar. Talking with Eleanor and showing off his sleeveless arms stood Crowell. He placed a hand on her shoulder and held up his glass to Dan.

"Easy friend," Crowell said. "I promise I'll pay you back somehow for what happened. I came to give my congratulations to you, and sympathies to your wife."

Dan pointed a finger to scold him again but broke out into laughter.

"I can't keep a grudge, you massive eyesore," Dan said and rubbed his wife's back, who continued to glare. "One little tiff won't break our friendship."

Sindrick made his way to the bar, pretending he was going to see Crowell. He didn't want to be obvious about getting closer to Eleanor. However, getting between the two of them was his primary goal.

"I blame Jack for it anyway," Crowell said. "If his drink didn't get us so smashed—" He paused and looked at Rena, who crossed her arms. "I mean, it was a terrible accident."

Sindrick wondered what Dan told his wife about the previous night. The redness growing on Rena's face told everyone of her aggravation.

"She doesn't like it when Dan goes drinking with us, remember?" Sindrick whispered to Crowell and pulled him away from Eleanor. "Did you bring a gift?"

Crowell looked around the room to everyone staring at him.

"Do you honestly believe I'd come to a party unprepared?" Crowell moved to the center of the room. "I'll need some help hauling it inside. Those who do will get the first taste."

He winked at Dan and made a grand exit out the door with a growing crowd close behind him.

Sindrick leaned back on the bar by Eleanor's side. She looked out the door with a distant gaze. In the dim light, the color of her green velvet dress reflected onto her eyes, like gems of emerald and citrine melded into perfect harmony. It seemed to create a spell Sindrick could not escape.

"Who was the muscle?" she asked. "I don't think he was around when we were young."

"That's Crowell, a good friend of mine," Sindrick said. "His family isn't from Virfell, and he comes and goes as he pleases. It wasn't too long ago when he started frequenting our town enough to call it home. It's sometimes good when he's back. But typically, it ends badly as you can guess."

"I see. Is he a craftsman as well?"

"Sailor. He only seems to show up when it's convenient for him to be around." Sindrick motioned for the barkeeper to pour them another round. "No one knows where he goes on his voyages. He has a fascination with the trolls, so we assume he's off hunting them."

"Vile things those trolls are." Eleanor nodded and took a slow drink from her glass. She appeared to be lost in thought. "Senseless creatures. They wiped out too many of us for no reason. I'd be happy to watch their island fall into the sea."

38

"I like to keep myself prepared. I've been fashioning weapons that can defeat any threat. You never know where our enemies may come from."

"The worst are the closest and unsuspecting." She turned to him and rubbed her hand on his arm. "You still don't remember when we met, do you?"

Sindrick looked into her eyes. He longed to remember someone like her and couldn't believe he would forget a woman so mesmerizing. His timing was always the worst when it came to relationships.

"After my mother died, things were very hard for my family." Sindrick turned to face the bar and took a heavy drink. "I always admired my father, but he was never the same after. He took the journey to the frozen hills not too long ago. Malek's helped me get things straightened out with the forge."

"I'm sorry to hear of your parents." Eleanor moved her hand to Sindrick's back. The warmth of it eased some of his tension. "Family is the most blessed of curses. Your father helped us with some quite remarkable items. I'd like to say I have them with me, but they were lost years ago."

Sindrick put his hand on hers, resting on the bar. Her skin felt stretched but velvety like her dress.

"I wish I could remember." He frowned. "I do not doubt that if you had stayed, we would know each other better."

"Maybe we can change our luck now." She smiled and leaned closer. "The fates have crossed our paths again for their own reasons."

Her hand twitched under his, and she quickly withdrew it. She grabbed the amulet around her neck. The blackened stone set in the center gave no reflection and captured the light around it.

"I shouldn't stay so late," she said abruptly. "Forgive me."

"Let me walk you to your lodging."

"It's no bother. I can keep myself safe." She turned to leave but then spun around and grabbed his arm. "I would like to see your forge. Is that possible?"

"Well, it's not mine, exactly." Sindrick swirled took a quick drink. "I'm working under Malek as his apprentice."

"I see." Her look of disapproval spoke more than the inflection in her words as she released him.

"It's not that I lack the skills to run a forge. My father taught me about blending elements before he left. I've learned some secrets about alchemy, which are quite impressive." Sindrick gestured with the cup, spilling some of its contents.

"Maybe you need more practice handling your drinks first." Eleanor laughed. "I'll be off."

"Wait, I can talk to Malek about having my own forge."

"You do what you must," she said and clasped his hand, shaking it firmly. "It was lovely talking with you, Sindrick. I hope we see each other soon."

Sindrick nodded, too confused to speak from her change of mood. He thought she wanted to know him as more than a friend, yet she walked out of the tavern as little more than a stranger. Whatever mysteries she hid of their past, he would likely never find out.

Her floral scent lingered at the bar. He rubbed the place on his arm where she touched him and shook his head to clear his thoughts.

"One for the journey," he told the barkeep and grabbed the bottle before the rest of the party arrived with Crowell's secret stash of rum.

Missing most of Dan's wedding had been bad enough, but not remembering someone like Eleanor caused his stomach to turn. He needed to dig through his memory to recount when they met. Doing so meant going through the grief of losing his mother again, a memory he spent many years working to forget.

4

Malek's large workshop had enough room to train multiple apprentices with one great forge at the center. Each anvil had helped many hopeful blacksmiths practice their skills throughout the years. The workload of the aging master was too much for him to do alone as Sindrick's father had done most of the commissions when they both owned the forge. And with the former group of apprentices moving away, Sindrick was the last remaining student.

The orders consistently streaming in allowed Sindrick little time to experiment with alchemy, his true passion. He was never good at managing his time, and Malek often caught him testing different theories while the work backed up. Combining metal gave him inspiration for more ideas.

He walked past his father's old anvil, gathering dust in the corner, and started working on a simple order for the day.

"So, this is where you've been hiding," a sweet voice floated over the sound of Sindrick's hammering. "I waited for you the past few nights to return to the tavern."

Eleanor stood at the doorway of the forge, her arm resting on the frame. The way the morning sun from outside silhouetted her form made Sindrick forget he was holding the end of a metal bar in the furnace, until the heat traveled up the rod and almost scorched his skin.

"Good to see you again." He pulled the rod out and laid it on the anvil, letting the white-hot metal cool to black. "It's been busy here. There are many wanting to replace their tools before the next season. I get distracted, so Malek has me working on the easier requests."

"You do realize that is not a very good excuse for keeping a woman waiting alone with her drink? One of your friends, Crowell the sailor, told me where you'd be." Eleanor stepped inside and ran her finger across the worn table of spare parts. "Honesty, this place is not bad. I remember when your father worked here. It was more focused on blending elements, not repairing farm tools. This looks closer to a typical smithery in an ordinary town."

43

"Malek likes to have it more business-minded and less of a place to expand the possibilities of alchemy." Sindrick motioned to the water near the door and made his way toward her. "Please, help yourself. I should probably take a break anyway."

"It's not as strong as I'd prefer, but thank you." Eleanor took a sip from the ladle and handed it to Sindrick. "I'm sure this place is warmer than the tavern at night."

"It is," Sindrick said and gulped down the water.

"I was hoping to get some insight on something." She palmed the dark medallion around her neck and looked out the door. The chain sparkled in the sunlight until it dimmed from a passing cloud. "I should probably ask the master since it's unlikely an apprentice would know how to unlock its power."

"I could do it," Sindrick said quickly. "Malek told me I'd surpassed him already."

"The whole reason I came to Virfell was to find your father. I guess there's no reason for me to stay if his son doesn't have his own place to practice."

"No, wait," Sindrick said as she started to leave. "I can create a new workshop at any time. I've learned how to study materials like my father."

"Is this true?" She looked at him playfully. "You know, if you had your own forge, we would have a private place to get away from everyone. Which is part of the reason I wanted to come here and catch you alone."

Sindrick's mind raced at the thought of being with her. "There's a lot of windows here, and Malek will be back soon. He went to buy food." He sighed and rubbed his chin to calm his nerves. "I'm not entirely sure if having two workshops in town would be worth it. I may need to set up in a different town."

"I'm sure you'll work something out." Eleanor nudged his arm. "I should be off. Certain things require my attention. I'll be gone for a while. Maybe it will give you enough time to get your own forge going."

"I'll see what I can do." Sindrick wiped the sweat from his brow. "If you don't mind me asking, where are you going?"

"I think I do mind." She raised an eyebrow and smiled. "Or I enjoy watching you guess. It's obvious you haven't been able to remember our childhood together. Give it time."

She exited before he could respond.

Sindrick wandered back to his station and tapped the anvil in the empty room. Having his own forge was something he aspired to, and there wasn't a good reason to keep him from building one, other than creating competition against his master.

The door swung open, and Sindrick briefly hoped it was Eleanor returning to tell him he wouldn't have to leave.

"You don't have to work so hard," Malek said, entering the room with a sack of vegetables over his shoulder. "I've been asking about the plows you made, and they turned out better than expected. There won't be many additional orders for us this season until winter ends. . . except for those who decide to work on ice."

"That is good news." Sindrick flicked a shard of wood into the flames, causing it to spark and crack. "Do you remember when I started my apprenticeship?"

"Your father didn't like bringing you around the forge until you were old enough to use the hammer with adequate strength." Malek sat down and placed the bag by his feet. "I always wondered why he waited so long to teach you."

"Some things are lost to the intents of the dead." Sindrick set his hammer next to the other tools he'd collected. "I remember seeing the pride in my father's eyes when the apprentices would leave Virfell, searching for a new place to build their forge. I wanted to have him see me the same way."

46

"He spoke of you often. You instantly picked up the skill, and you had an eye for those special abilities hidden to me. I told him you would pass up the lot of us and become a master alchemist instead of a blacksmith." Malek sighed. "I suppose this is why you're packing your tools. I've seen the look of wanderlust before."

"Do you think I'm ready to build my own forge?"

"You were always ready, before your father left this world," Malek said and helped Sindrick gather his belongings. "I'm thankful for your company, but know you have likely taught me more than I have instructed you. Your father is in the heat of the forge. Every time you strike the anvil, his strength is shown through you."

"His strength didn't save my mother."

Sindrick regretted letting the words slip out. His father had tried everything. It happened too suddenly.

"There are some tragedies no manner of strength or magic can save." Malek placed a hand on Sindrick's chest. "We must save their memories in our hearts and in our passion for life."

"I know," Sindrick said. "I'm ready to pursue something greater. It's time to build my workshop."

The master stroked his beard. It curled in strange directions from the heat of the forge.

"There will be no way for me to change your mind," Malek said at last. "I know that running your own forge is a task you can diligently perform, but starting a business will require more of you than you can imagine. Do not take this path lightly."

Sindrick wanted to respond but chose to remain silent. He nodded instead and continued to wrap his tools together.

"If you were to set up a new forge, where would you build it?" Sindrick asked.

"There have been settlements growing in the north. They often require weapons to defend themselves from the creatures who come down from the frozen hills. Their soil is also harder, so they need better tools to break up the land. Someone with your abilities would be a great benefit."

"Thank you. I will look there first."

Sindrick paused to stare into the fire of the forge. His desire to leave had been growing before the mysterious woman in the tavern gave him the motivation. Eleanor, the one he almost remembered.

She had the same expression of wonder Sindrick remembered seeing in his mother's eyes. His father liked to say that his passion for metals started because of his wife when they were still courting. She admired every detail and helped keep the forge burning.

Sindrick stepped out onto the streets, following a similar path his father first took in creating the greatest forge in Virfell. Having someone by his side would make all the difference. He hoped Eleanor would be the spark for his new life, but he would need to find a place to build.

5

After venturing the long road to one of the northern towns, Sindrick's dream proved to be more of a task than he expected. Most of the shops were full of new businesses, and the lodging for travelers was in high demand, so they took top coin. The offer of the ruby sword was enough to convince Crowell to help him set up, but promises wouldn't be enough for the new villagers.

Crowell also wanted an opportunity to practice some of his summoning spells in the frozen hills. His eagerness to do so outweighed his desire for the new blade. Luckily, one of the residents had room in a small shack.

It took persuasion from both of them to get Sindrick settled into the simple shelter at the edge of town, which was located between two mountain passes. It wouldn't be long until the roads would close from the snow and ice howling down the banks, making the rush to set up the forge more urgent.

"Are you sure you're fit enough to stay here?" Crowell asked, dropping down the bag of supplies. "It's going to be brutal come winter. I've told you before, you should take up a bunk on my ship. We've got a few to spare, and I likely won't be leaving for a while."

"I'll be able to survive. Once I find the right space for a forge, I'll have the warmest place in town." Sindrick found an indentation in the wall to build a fire. The hole above it had been boarded up. "Besides, you're always saying you'll be around, and then you vanish onto the next port before anyone notices."

"What? You don't want to wake up in an exotic land somewhere far from this frozen wasteland?" Crowell laughed. "Truthfully, I may be leaving soon. It seems like the weather is getting worse each year. Don't want to be trapped in an ice box when I could be enjoying the company of warmer folks."

"I assumed as much."

Sindrick grabbed a pole and rammed the board, knocking it loose to let any smoke out. Shards of the old wood fell into his hair.

"If I fail here, I might have no choice but to join your crew," he said. "Thank you for helping me haul my things."

"Not a bother at all. You'd do the same, and have done more when I was getting things set for my first voyage from Virfell if you recall. Don't get me wrong, I don't work for free. I am expecting my new sword to be done before the next time I set sail."

"If you stick around long enough, I might add some embellishments to it." Sindrick tapped Crowell with the pole.

"Your idle promises might work better once I see the piece," Crowell said and batted the pole out of Sindrick's hands. "I know your reasons for wanting me to come and help."

"You do?" Sindrick acted like he didn't know what Crowell was about to say. He hoped his feelings for Eleanor weren't too noticeable.

"You've got some unfulfilled destiny toward your family legacy. Being a forge master runs in your veins. Working the metal is about all you do best."

Sindrick let out the breath he was holding in. "It's an honest living."

"And you want me far away from that special woman you were eyeing in the bar." He winked.

"She's an old friend." Sindrick wished he could remember how she was an old friend. "She grew up Virfell. My father helped her family."

"You don't need to worry about me around her." Crowell looked out the window. "There's nothing she has that would suit my needs."

Sindrick noticed him rubbing the chain around his neck. It had a similar color to it as the one on Eleanor's amulet. The metals blended together the same.

"Your necklace is new, where did you get it?" he asked.

"This?" Crowell pulled out the solitary chain from under his shirt. "I've had it for a while." He turned to Sindrick's inquisitive look. "That is to say, I've had it since I visited Raikrune. Do you see something hidden in it?"

"It looks the same as—" Sindrick stopped himself.

Crowell burst into a laugh and tucked it away. "You noticed it was the same as your lady's, right? I thought they were similar as well when I spoke with her at the tavern."

"She was quite impressed by my father's work." Sindrick smiled and stuck his chest out.

"So, she's the reason you're starting your forge?"

Matthew E. Nordin

"No, no," Sindrick lied to convince himself he had deeper motives. "It was time for me to move on. Malek told me I'd been ready before I mentioned it to him."

"Whatever you say, master," Crowell said and gave a mocking bow. "Shall I prepare a fire for you?"

"I'll take care of the heat in here." Sindrick pushed his friend back up. "Can you scavenge for something resembling a table? I want to get our things off the ground. The warmth will likely bring out whatever's been living under these boards." He pointed to the mouse holes chewed through the walls.

"I'll fashion a few ropes for a hammock while I'm at it. If you ever come to your senses and join my crew, at least you'll know how to sleep properly, even with the other rats." Crowell wandered into a spare room.

"Does that make you the king of the rats?" Sindrick called to him. "Once I find a permanent place for the forge, I should be set. Location is key to a successful shop. If I'm too far away from this town, no one will come to me for requests. But if I'm too close, the noise of the forge will cause complaints. And I don't want people tempted to take any of the gems I use. As you know, some are quite valuable."

54

"All of the ones I smuggled for you, you mean?" Crowell said, returning with a large flattened stump. He grunted as he sat it down in the middle of the room. "You know, we could use rope to hang your things. It'd be more secure than this rotting chunk of wood. Anything could crawl up it."

"Good point," Sindrick said with a smile. "You can move the stump back."

Crowell started to bend down, but straightened up and shook his finger at Sindrick. "Hey, you're not my master. This can stay here for all I care." He chuckled to himself. "Maybe you and the girl will get along well."

"I'm hoping we do," Sindrick said as Crowell reluctantly rolled the log back where he found it.

Sindrick grabbed a flat rock from his bag and a glass-encased gem on top of it. He broke the glass from the stone with a sharp strike near the fireplace. It instantly lit into a blue flame.

Using his hammer to prod it in, he slid it under a pile of logs and let it ignite them. Smoke trailed up the chimney and out of the home.

"That's quite an impressive concoction you've developed," Crowell said, tying knots in the rope to create a net.

"When you're up early to work, the creativity happens. Once I discovered the catalyst gem to be common in this area, the rest was easy." Sindrick placed the hammer in his bag of tools and rummaged through his other belongings.

"I'd like to learn some of your tricks after I've mastered a few more summoning spells." Crowell moved closer to the fire. "They say the beasts come from the abyss of the ocean depths, but I'm betting others are lurking in the untouched hills farther north."

"You have a knack for those spells. I've tried looking through some magic books when I was a child. They don't make much sense to me."

"Best leave it to us gifted ones. You'd probably start talking to trees like the elves if you tried anything beyond rocks."

"If I could make the log light itself with a word, that would be impressive." Sindrick pulled out his cooking gear. "All I do is allow the metal to speak to me in its hidden patterns. I'm like an observer."

"On second thought, maybe you should keep your secrets to yourself. I don't want you teaching me something I wouldn't have control over."

Crowell stretched out the net, tying one end of it to an exposed wall beam. He pressed down on it, carefully eyeing the walls and roof.

"It'll hold," Sindrick assured him. "Tompkins said this place has lasted for at least two generations."

"But our host probably never had anyone of my size in here before." Crowell smiled. "I've broken quite a few chairs, but my knots will stay true. I'm more worried about the structure."

Sindrick ran a hand across the dirt-packed boards on the floor. "You shouldn't be. I had a curious feeling about this place. It's like the wood and rocks have woven together."

"Whatever you say." Crowell reclined on his hammock. "If you don't mind, I need to rest a while before we eat. I'd like to go out tonight to try the summoning spells. They always seem to work better in the dark."

"Do you need me to pack you some of my fire stones?"

"I'll be fine without them. I've weathered harsher climates. Not having the sea spray freezing across me is a blessing. You've never been cold until you've experienced the northern seas around here."

"I can imagine." Sindrick placed another log on the fire. "I'll get a stew brewing. It'll be a while before it's ready, and I probably won't eat much. I've got too much on my mind."

Crowell grunted and closed his eyes. Before long, he was snoring.

Sindrick snuck out with a small kettle to collect some snow for melting. He noticed the sunlight creating long shadows across the barren countryside as it hovered low near the horizon. The shack was a good place to observe the perimeter of the town. Although too close to do any real forging, he could create a few simple tools to help pay for a permanent site.

He quietly reentered his temporary residence and unrolled the food they had prepared for their journey. The pleasant scent kept him awake while the water boiled to make the meat tender. Although he was hungrier than he suspected, there would be plenty of leftovers for Crowell, whenever the beast decided to rise.

6

The young blacksmith woke up alone in the warm shack the next morning. Crowell had disappeared late in the night and hadn't returned. However, the captain often snuck off, sometimes for days on end.

Sindrick was eager to visit with the owner of the shelter they were staying in. Tompkins would give him needed insight on the northern village. From what he learned, there were a few shops to choose from for a forge. Yet, they came at a steep price, and he would be paying for them long into old age.

He knocked on Tompkins' door, hoping the landlord would guide him in the right direction.

"Come in," the older man said as he swung open the door. Although not as old as Malek, Tompkins had streaks of gray throughout his long hair and beard.

"We've finished setting up the table," his wife called out from the other room. "I suspected you and your friend might be coming over sometime today, so we prepared a hearty breakfast for you. I hope you don't have much to do today."

Sindrick took the kind gesture without hesitation and rushed inside to the aroma of wild turkey and boar meat. The northern herbs carried a richer flavor, giving a bold spice to everything. He could almost taste the pepper and lemon scent in the air.

"I'd like to go into further detail about the arrangement for your stay," Tompkins said after Sindrick settled at the chair across from him. "You mentioned you were looking for a location to set up a permanent shop. Being your hosts, we are going to worry about you wandering into some of the abandoned buildings around the town. Not all of them are safe."

"I trust your judgment and hope to find something simple but sturdy," Sindrick said as the host's wife scooped some of the seasoned meat into his bowl. "Sadly, I'm not sure any in town will suit the needs of a forge."

"Would you build your own place?" The man took a deep slurp of the food already before him at the table.

"I might have to, but having an existing framework would help. Do you know of any place secluded from the town that isn't too far to walk?"

"There is an old farmstead up the hill." Tompkins reclined back and broke off a piece of bread. "Not much was done to it once the owner discovered the area had large patches of hard stone and metal. After we eat, I can take you there if you like. It's not too far."

"Thank you, but I should look at it alone. It will give me time to observe the materials around the area."

"A man of stone and seclusion, admirable. It would also be better for my family if you go on your own. We need to do some hunting today to stock up for winter." Tompkins leaned in and motioned for Sindrick to get closer. "The path is marked by a blue post at the west edge of town. If you know what to look for, you can't miss it. Keep an eye out after a few miles. The old home blends in with the plants growing around it."

"I'll keep my eyes open." Sindrick grabbed a hunk of meat and scarfed it down. The grainy peppers stuck in his teeth. "I could use the walk after all this tasty food. Thank you for hosting us."

"The promise of a blacksmith up here was enough for me," Tompkins said and pointed a spoon at him. "Of course, my wife will want a full payment when you're done staying in our guest home."

Her mouth was too full of food to make an audible comeback. She smiled and nodded.

"If you go too far on the path, you'll reach the sea," Tompkins continued. "There are too many cliffs for a harbor, but there are plenty of unique rocks and stones tucked away in the coves. No one farms out there because the ground is practically sitting on a solid metal deposit, perfect for the forge you're looking to build."

"Do you know who owns the land?" Sindrick's eyes got wide just thinking about the limitless supply of gems created from the sea's corrosion and rock formations.

"I would be able to work out a deal with the town for you. The last owner passed to the frozen hills many seasons ago. The place has sat abandoned since then, and no one's wanted to fix it up. It needs a lot of work."

"I can imagine," Sindrick said. "Would it be okay if I stayed there overnight?"

"It wouldn't be wise to set up camp in the building without supplies, but that may be my joints talking." Tompkins laughed.

"I'm not as young as you to be running up the path and battling a cold night."

"There have been some harsh nights I've weathered through, but I prefer a proper fire to keep warm. From what you're saying, I can get there and back before nightfall."

"I can at least show you where the path begins to go out of town. Don't want you wandering the trails aimlessly. Most of the roads lead to the northern hills in the forgotten lands."

Sindrick took a slow drink of the fruity liquid Tompkins had prepared for him. He hoped Crowell hadn't wandered too far from the town. He was missing out.

His worries subsided from a slap on the back from Tompkins, signaling their departure. The host's cheerfulness calmed his spirit while they ventured into the streets.

A door was propped over the opening to the lone building in the west, exactly where Tompkins described it. The metal hinges had fallen away, and the slab fixed itself against the entrance.

Sindrick picked at the deteriorating wood around the frame. He could craft a more durable material to protect against the spray misting off the sea. Enough of a gap allowed Sindrick to peek inside the building. Most of the roof remained intact, but the windows had weathered away like the door frame.

"In need of some work was an understatement," he muttered to himself.

Sindrick grabbed the heavy door and tried to pull it back, but it didn't budge. The salt in the air had hardened into a permanent seal. It would be impossible to dislodge without the right tools.

He kicked at the small openings at the bottom, enough space to get a boot through but not for his whole body.

Sindrick tried again to free the door from the bottom, but it shook the whole structure from the force.

"What a piece of—" a rodent rushed out of the opening before he could finish.

He laughed at his startled reaction and kicked the door one last time.

"I'll get back to you soon," he said and pointed at the entrance.

He ran his hands through his hair and leaned back to get a view of the place. It would be big enough to hold a forge, and he could set up a small area in front to sell things. It wouldn't be as large as the one his father and Malek used, but he didn't need space to train apprentices. He would stay busy searching for new materials, and his living room would be the sea.

The idea of wandering down the path to view the water was tempting, but the sun had already begun its descent. Crawling into the window to set up camp didn't sound like a good idea, especially without any supplies or protection from the small creatures inside. He would need to return to the town.

The fog grew thick as he traveled down the hill to get back. Hopefully, Crowell would have returned from his endeavors and cooked some food. The long journey had burned off much of Sindrick's strength, and he was grateful for the generous meal from his hosts. Living on his own in Virfell made those types of feasts a rarity.

Subtle hints of the smoked boar lingered in the air as Sindrick neared the guest home. Night had already settled in, and it became difficult to continue down the road in the darkness. The alluring smell changed into a horrific sight.

The fog lifted enough for Sindrick to make out remains of the shelter he had been staying in.

Boards were scattered around the area as if something exploded inside. A small glow from the dying coals of the fire cast strange shadows over the wreckage. Whatever happened was fast and left little behind.

Sindrick found scraps of his supply bag. His tools were warped or missing pieces, and his hammer had shattered in half from the blast.

A noise from behind caused him to whirl around.

Something reached out to grab him, but he feigned back and countered with a quick jab. His hand hit a stiff object of fur and bone. The crack of the blow caused his hand to ache.

Before he could get a second attempt, he was shoved off balance.

He toppled to the ground and frantically scrambled for an object to defend himself. His fingers slid across a bar, and he swung it toward his assailant.

It stopped short.

Someone knocked back his hand and crouched in front of him quickly—Crowell. His eyes were wild with fear and anger.

"What are you doing?" Crowell whispered and shook the bar loose. "You nearly took my head off."

"Me?" Sindrick stood up. "What happened to the shack?"

The Salty Eleanor

"Keep it down," Crowell said in a hushed voice and pulled Sindrick back to his level. "There's something out there. I only wounded it."

Sindrick looked around the chaos of the ruined building. There didn't seem to be a visible threat of anything beyond the debris.

"You haven't answered my question," he whispered. "What happened here?"

"I. . . I thought it would kill it." Crowell rubbed his hands together and wrapped his fur coat tighter over his shoulders. Something caused him to tremble more than the cold. "There was a beast." He smiled. "I was right about summoning creatures on land."

"Do you have control over any of your spells?"

"They told me I would as I got stronger, but those birds were not in my power. I figured whatever I summoned wouldn't try to attack me." His smile faded, and he looked toward the north. "I was wrong. The creature from the frozen hills appeared to be small and docile. It didn't move at first, and I wasn't certain it was alive. I assumed it needed a little prodding to get going."

"What did you do to the shack?" Sindrick grabbed the bar again.

67

"I'm getting to that," Crowell said sharply. "It yanked the stick from me and tossed it to the side. The force from its throw stuck the branch deep into the ice on a cliff face. That's when I knew something was wrong. I tried to get away from it, but it kept growing and getting faster. I managed to lure it inside the shack. Luckily, I brought some explosives with me. You never know when you'll need them. I didn't have time to get our stuff out before lighting up the creature. Sorry."

"I'm glad you didn't end up like everything else around here." Sindrick let the bar loose, and a small cloud of ash rose where it landed. "You said it might be alive. How could anything survive the blast?"

"I saw something run north. I think what happened scared it off, but I'm not sure it's dead. I thought you were the beast returning, until I got closer. You should be happy I didn't have any extra powder with me. I would've tossed first."

"Thank you for thinking of me," Sindrick said and nudged Crowell's arm. "The owner is going to be furious. What should we tell him?"

"I'm going to hide out here to make sure the creature is not following me. Once I'm convinced it's safe, I'm heading back to

Virfell. This whole trip was your idea. You can inform Tompkins of what happened if you like. Maybe he'll let you stay with him."

"You're going to drop this on me?" Sindrick wanted to be angry at Crowell, but the fear in his eyes made him look insane.

"It's not worth the risk," Crowell said quietly.

Sindrick sighed and kicked at the fallen boards. Tompkins' family would be returning from their hunt soon. The best way to break the news to them would be if he had enough money to pay for the damage. Everything he owned was mixed with the scattered rubble. A sense of dread filled him.

"I shouldn't be seen here either," Sindrick said as he searched for any salvageable items. He found a blanket without any holes and fashioned it into a cloak with one of the metal pins sticking out of the ground. "I'm heading back to Virfell now. Did you want to come with me?"

"No. I need to make sure the creature doesn't return. I'll remain out of sight." Crowell untied a small bag from his belt and tossed it to Sindrick. "Take this with you. It should get you by."

Sindrick opened the bag to find some broken pieces of bread and cheese. "Thanks. Sorry for almost taking your head off."

"You wouldn't stand a chance against me in a real fight." Crowell chuckled softly and crept away into the night, disappearing in the fog.

Sindrick shoved a fistful of food into his mouth before securing the bag onto his belt. Somehow he would find a way to repay Tompkins for the damage or convince Crowell to pay for it. He quietly jogged down the main road leading back to Virfell and did not turn to look back.

7

"Does this mean the hopeless dreamer has returned?" Jack called across the tavern. He made his way over to the table where Sindrick sat, holding his cup halfway to his mouth.

Sindrick placed his drink down. He had been pondering over Crowell's tale of the beast he discovered. There would be no way for him to return north with what happened to Tompkins' guest home.

"I don't blame you," Jack continued and pulled an extra chair over. "I couldn't handle being alone with Crowell either. He's been acting progressively strange with each journey. I'm surprised you let him go with you. He didn't try recruiting you to his crew, did he?"

"You know him, he's persistent. It always comes up. I would've asked you to come with me, but I assumed Kate would have none of it." Sindrick rested his arms on the table and leaned forward. "I owe you a lot for the different chemicals you've let me use with my alchemy, but I could use your help covering this round."

"With the way you've been fiddling with your drink, I figured something happened. What did he do?"

"He did what he does best." Sindrick shook his head. "I should've stayed and explained to our hosts what happened. Crowell blew up the guest house because of a creature he summoned in the hills. I panicked. I wanted to stay and pay for it, but everything I owned was destroyed."

"Are you serious?" Jack raised his eyebrows with a concerned look. "I knew there was something evil with his spells. I'll get this one for you. Do you have a place to stay?"

"I should be able to stay with Malek. I'll have to forge another set of tools anyway."

The realization of having to start over made Sindrick sink back in his chair. No one would want to be with him, especially Eleanor.

The Salty Eleanor

He took a few sips of his drink. The bitter grains overpowered any sweet notes of honey trying to make it tolerable to anyone other than the locals. It made him feel at home.

"You'll endure this trial quick enough." Jack folded his arms and sat back. "I was hoping you wouldn't ask to stay with me because Kate has been over more often. It's hard enough keeping one person a secret from the brewmaster." He tapped his nose and smiled. "So, where did the great captain end up?"

"He wanted to make sure the creature didn't follow him back here. He'll probably turn up like he does, at the most inconvenient time."

"You're the one who does that." Jack laughed. "The girl you like showed up last night, asking about you. She said she returned from a short trip."

"I never said I liked her," Sindrick said and tried to keep from blushing.

"It would be wise not to get close to her," Jack said and looked into his drink. "I've met plenty of girls like her before I found Kate. Love is never enough. Best to enjoy whatever happens and move on. Nothing but trouble and scars."

"Why would you say that? She's got more class than anyone else in Virfell."

73

"The look in her eyes." Jack stuck his hands under his arms. "Whatever she's after gave me more of a chill than the winter Dan made us those special trousers. I swear those let in more air than our bare skin."

"Nearly got frostbite in places no one should get it," Sindrick said with a smirk.

Jack slapped his thigh and took a quick swig of his drink. "I could be wrong about her. But it doesn't help with where she bunked up in town."

"Where?"

"An older family south of town took her in. She said her family was good friends with them." Jack paused with a blissful gaze. "This community never ceases to surprise me. I'm finding out there's always something new happening."

"It would be nice to be closer to the larger cities," Sindrick said more to himself. "With the lack of trade here, no one seems to stick around for long. I suppose most people enjoy the warmer climate. This weather isn't for everyone."

"If you ask me, it's not for anyone. We just suffer through it, a bit crazy that way."

"It's probably too cold for most of us to move." Sindrick laughed. "Anyway, do you know which couple took in Eleanor? There are a few elderly people living in the south."

"I can't say I remember their names. They're the ones with all sorts of bones and dead animals in their home."

"Ah, I know who you're speaking of. Malek's been trying to sell them stuff for years. They're hard customers. They won't buy anything that's not made from an animal."

"I don't trust those types of people." Jack put his foot on the table. "Kate is always going on about how we need to respect every creature. I'm beginning to agree with her rhetoric, or I was for a while. I can never keep up with what she believes about things."

"I am surprised Eleanor would be staying with them." Sindrick rocked his chair against the wall on its back legs. "I've heard those two can be cruel, especially to pets."

"Wait, are those the people Dan was talking about when he said their dogs went missing?"

"Those are the ones." Sindrick peered outside the window.

Although he stopped for the night on the journey back, the afternoon sun was making him drowsy. A slight chill pierced the air, but no clouds blocked any of the light from illuminating the tavern. He rocked forward and took a long drink.

"Wouldn't she be bothered by the dead animals?" Sindrick asked.

"Maybe." Jack shrugged. "I would feel ill-at-ease there. She asked where you were when I saw her earlier, but I wasn't sure. You left without telling anyone your destination. People around here started to worry."

"I promise I'll let you know if I leave again." Sindrick winked at him. "Wouldn't want you getting all worried about me."

"You know what I mean. I've got problems too, and no one else listens to them. At least you don't walk away when I go on about them."

"Now you know the real reason I left for the north," Sindrick teased. "I should probably leave here soon, though. I want to check on Eleanor to make sure she's okay, and I'm a bit worried about returning to Malek's forge. I told him I was ready to start on my own and failed miserably."

"Whatever you decide to do, please let me know about it," Jack said. "Regardless of what you think about yourself, you have people here who care about your well-being. Not saying I'm one of them, but I'm sure Crowell would beat himself up about it."

Jack stood up and slapped Sindrick's back.

"You take care of yourself as well." Sindrick finished off his drink. "Don't hit the bottle too hard. If Kate's sneaking into your room more often, you need to have all your wits about you."

Jack nodded and wandered back to the barkeep.

Sindrick frowned at the thought of Jack and Kate being together. He knew they were right for each other, but it also meant that his times with Jack would become less.

With any luck, Sindrick could have a constant companion of his own. It never seemed so real of a possibility to him until he met Eleanor. There were some he had fallen for in the village, but none quite so hard or so sudden. The others seemed to be minor stops along his path to love. He needed to find her and see if she could be his last.

Although the houses in Virfell were similar in size and material, this one in particular was plain. No one would assume it out of the ordinary if not for the littering of fur and a bone fence leading up to the door. On closer look, reflective eyes glared out the windows to any passerby. The wolves propped up on the other side were busts of the creatures and meant to scare off uninvited guests.

Sindrick took a deep breath and remained on the other side of the fence, tapping it lightly to calm his nerves. The couple inside was extremely reclusive. They didn't seem like the company Eleanor would want to keep.

"You're too far to turn back," Sindrick muttered to himself and continued to walk to the door.

The boards leading up to it screeched out to alert anyone of a visitor. If the couple was anything like the rumors, he should've brought a weapon.

The stuffed creatures in the window seemed to move as shadows shifted between the cracks in the log cabin.

"Hello?" Sindrick called out. "I've come to meet a friend. Is Eleanor here?"

The door remained closed, and no one responded. Sindrick knocked on the old and dusty door.

"This is Sindrick," he said after a silence. "I'm the blacksmith's apprentice."

He knocked again, but the shuffling near the door never returned. Giving a heavy sigh, he turned back down the path with his head down. Jack had never been one to provide false information, even if he liked to embellish on the truth.

"What are you doing out here?" Eleanor asked, almost running into him. She gripped the shovel she carried close to her. "I thought you went north to work on a forge with Crowell or something."

"I had to return." Sindrick looked up briefly. "There was an accident, and the place was destroyed, including my tools."

"Crowell's not with you, is he?" Eleanor glanced behind her.

"No. He's the one who caused it."

"Sounds like you could use some help rebuilding." Eleanor placed the shovel on the fence and stretched her back. "Why did you come back so fast?"

"I offered to stay and help," Sindrick lied. He didn't want her to know that he fled like a coward. "Our hosts said they were okay, and I should hurry to Virfell so I can get more supplies before the pass freezes over."

"You never answered my question from before," she said and put a hand on her hip. The dirt on her hands smeared across her tan skirt. "What are you doing here?"

Her mesmerizing stare made his heart increase its pounding.

"I was hoping to see you," he managed to say.

"Here I am." She held her arms out. "What were you going to do after that?"

Sindrick smiled and had no idea what to say. The sunlight reflecting off her skin and tiredness from his journey made him feel like he was floating in a dream.

"I've been wondering why you choose the north," she continued. "Wouldn't they have enough metal workers up there for the ice?"

"From what our host said, there wasn't any. They wouldn't know how to blend the metals like I do anyway. There are rare ones no one has bothered to research along the coves. It would be wonderful to see what properties they possessed."

"What do you mean properties?" She scoffed. "Isn't hard or soft the main ones?"

"It can be. Certain elements can be more brittle than others. But once you align them together, they can exhibit other abilities."

"Interesting." Eleanor leaned against the fence post and gave a sly smile. "Please, go on."

"Each material has a different trait waiting to be discovered— plows made to help the soil produce food easier, swords imbued to protect the wielder, and decorations which light themselves. I found one combination that instantly combusts without flint or tinder."

"You can discern the different properties of items by sight alone?"

"Exactly." Sindrick sat beside her on the fence. "There is a certain feeling I get about them, more of an intuition. My father called it alchemy. It was an innate ability within me."

Eleanor looked around and took off the amulet around her neck. "You are the one I'm looking for then. Would you be able to read this stone? I acquired it recently and know it is rare."

Sindrick took the amulet and held it up to get a better view. The dark gem absorbed the light around it and cast no shadow on the ground, void of any physical property he could distinguish. No patterns formed in the chaotic abyss of the material.

"Where did you get something like this?" Sindrick turned it over to reveal more of the pitch blackness. "It is beautiful."

"You wouldn't believe me if I told you," she said and held her hand out.

"It feels like a hole through reality, like a window into another world."

Sindrick reluctantly gave the amulet back to Eleanor. The materials need to be studied further. It could be tested with other chemicals to bring out its hidden traits—unlike anything he had ever seen before.

81

"Please, I must know." Sindrick couldn't hide his curiosity. "Where is it from?"

"The elven woods," she whispered and slipped it back around her neck. "A group of scavengers told me they recovered it from a hidden structure before the building crumbled. A sorcerer of great power built it without the elves knowing. Once they discovered it, the citadel was destroyed. This piece is one of the few remnants."

"I would love exploring the elven island with you." Sindrick wrung his wrists. "I wish you could have seen the village with me in the north. The place I found was perfect and close to the sea. But I doubt I'll ever get enough to purchase it, especially now."

"What other things can you create with your ability to change metal?" she asked, scooting closer to him.

"I suppose there is no limit to what can be enchanted or molded together. Some called my father a magician, but I always understood it was more of an understanding of the natural world. Alchemy is more physical than mystical."

"I see." She kicked her boots on the ground, leaving streaks of mud and grass. The land was not completely frozen yet, but a hint of ice graced the air. "Yes." She nudged him with her shoulder.

"What do you mean?" Sindrick braced himself from toppling off the fence.

The Salty Eleanor

"You said you wished I could travel north with you." She brushed her hair back. "My answer is yes. I would like to come. The place by the sea sounds like a perfect place for you to set up your workshop and study my amulet."

Sindrick's cheeks turned warm. "It would take some time to get the money for it, and I'm not sure it would be best for the two of us to go up there alone. Wouldn't you need to tell the couple you are staying with?"

Eleanor looked at the house behind them. "The people here are strange."

"It's not that I don't want to be with you. Our town doesn't like it when unwed people move in together, especially the old folks who live here from what I've heard." Sindrick frowned. "I suppose we could move there after the winter."

"Or we could leave before they realize I'm gone. I already have a cart ready from my last trip."

"Let's go!" Sindrick blurted out. The realization that he had no belongings made him grab Eleanor's arm. "Wait. My things were destroyed, and I have nothing to pay for the building."

"Don't worry," she said and took his hand into hers. "I will take care of things when we get there. You need more tools, right?"

"Yeah." Sindrick sighed.

"Use this to get what you need." Eleanor reached into her bag.

She gave him a handful of coins, more than enough to pay for a new set. Sindrick had to count them again. It was the average wage for an entire season.

"How did you—" Sindrick began, but Eleanor put a finger to his lips before he could finish.

The determination in her eyes caused his worries to subside.

"No more questions, only action." She brushed down her garments. "I'll need to change out of these dirty clothes and pack a few other items. Let's meet at the tavern. And hurry. The barkeep has been saying things about me, and none of them are true. I don't care too much for the company there either."

Sindrick nodded and rushed back to Malek's workshop. He didn't understand why Eleanor wanted to start their new life together already, but he wouldn't protest.

It took little convincing to get the tools he needed with the number of coins he gave to his former master. After reclining at one of the booths in the tavern, he found himself fading into sleep, waiting for Eleanor to join his return to the north.

8

The sun had already set when Eleanor shook Sindrick out of his slumber to begin their journey. With her by his side, the trip became an enjoyable adventure. He tried to delve more into her past, but Eleanor avoided questions about herself. She continued to ask him what happened to his family.

Although painful to recount, he understood why his father left for the frozen hills. After his mother died, nothing was the same anymore. His father's will to live faded away.

"You keep wondering about my family but never talk about yours," Sindrick said as they sat together on the horse-drawn cart.

"There's not much to say," Eleanor said and huddled closer. The temperature continued to drop in the night. "I don't get along with them. As soon as I was able to leave, I did. Traveling around and seeing new places was nice, but there's something special about where you grew up. No matter where you go, you have to remember your roots."

Sindrick wrapped his arm around her. "I suppose that would be true if I ever left. This is about as far as I've gone."

"We should take a trip with your sailor friend someday." Eleanor shivered next to him and rubbed her arms.

"You're not enjoying this journey?" Sindrick smiled as they rounded the corner between the mountains. A blast of cold air blew into his face, almost freezing his nostrils shut. "It will be nice once we get the new forge set up. I'll keep it burning so we should stay plenty warm all winter."

"Maybe we should stop for the night. I need something now to keep from freezing."

Sindrick nodded and led the horses to a small enclave that blocked the howling wind.

"It would be better to go through town in the morning, anyway," he said. "I'll set up camp."

After loosening the firewood from the cart, he lit them near the cliff face with one of his fire stones. Eleanor wrapped herself in more of the blankets and sat near the flames.

"I hope you didn't tell anyone where we were going. I need some time alone with you," she said while Sindrick stretched out the tent. "It's funny, my parents told me to get their blessing before moving in with anyone. Not that I care, but I think they would have given it to you." She sighed. "I grew close to your family as a child, but you didn't seem to notice me."

"I'm sorry, I can't remember." Sindrick's hands grew numb while he tied the ropes to give the canvas a small structure close to the warmth of the fire. "I wish I would have been able to convince your family to stay. We could've gotten to know each other more growing up. I guess we'll have to make up for the lost time."

"Yes, we will." She stood up and piled the blankets into the tent.

Sindrick wandered closer to the fire and put a couple more logs onto it. His alchemical stone would keep them producing a steady flame. If he found the right materials, he could create heat without the use of wood. His forge would be able to burn without fuel.

"Aren't you going to join me?" Eleanor asked, causing Sindrick to break his trance with the flames.

"I should—" His throat dried up, and he had to clear it. "I mean, someone should stay out here and keep watch. There could be bandits or other travelers who could see us."

Eleanor walked up to him and ran her fingers across the back of his neck. She traced them around his face.

"There's no one out here but the stars," she whispered.

They reflected in her eyes as she led him into the tent. She closed the opening and pulled him close. Her lips pressed against his, and they kept each other warm the rest of the night.

The hills rose to the plateau where the lone building rested before the cliffs dropped off into the sea. The roof blended in with the rest of the surroundings from years of neglect. If it hadn't been found earlier, they would have never noticed it.

After a couple of hits with a hammer and a board to pry it open, the door came loose.

"Well, it's not as big as Malek's shop, but it will work," Sindrick said to coax Eleanor inside.

She had a concerned look on her face and remained near the cart.

"We can add on if we need to," he continued. "It might be cramped for a while until things get situated."

"This will be perfect," Eleanor said with a happier expression as she walked inside. "It won't take much to fix it up. We could set up an area by the door to sell things. Tompkins got us a reasonable price for this place, but we'll need to get an alternative income soon. I should be able to get some of the money back if I —" She trailed off in her thoughts and then rushed to the far wall. "Look, here's a great place to set up the forge."

She pointed to a small indentation in the wall resembling a shoddy fireplace. The one in the destroyed shack had been in better shape.

"We won't have much room for a bed," Sindrick said. "If we build a counter to sell things in the front, the forge and workspace will take up most of the back area."

"We don't need a big bed anyway." She gave him a wink. "I'll get a space cleared if you want to get our things."

Sindrick went back out to grab their supplies and started to shake. He wished it was from the cold, but he had never been close to anyone before, especially someone like Eleanor. Her passions were fierce. It would be hard to focus on anything else. Whatever she asked of him, he would do for her.

"I should get a fire going soon," Sindrick said, returning with an armful of the boxes Eleanor brought with them. "We'll want to keep our things off the ground for a while. Crowell showed me a few tricks with fashioning ropes."

"I hope he made it back to Virfell in one piece. From what you said, it sounded like he was pretty shaken up." Eleanor grabbed some of the rubble she collected and tossed it out an open window. "Are we safe up here?"

"We should be fine. Half of what he says is a fabrication of his imagination." Sindrick set the load down. "Can you help me with the anvil and parts for the forge? I'd like to get it set up right away."

Eleanor nodded, and they helped each other unload the cart. Sindrick tied knots for suspended shelves while Eleanor continued to throw out remnants from the previous owners. Some debris required both of them to heave it out the window. Taking care of the exterior would be something to worry about once they had the inside ready.

"I'm going to set up our bedroom," Eleanor said. "This work is making me tired."

"I understand." Sindrick grabbed their pile of blankets and walked to the opposite wall, dropping them near it. "You can put it here. I'll mark off how much space I need for my crafting."

He walked out a few paces and laid down sticks to mark off the room. One of the first things he would need to construct would be a table to examine and test the metals. The anvil would need to be near the wall so it wouldn't be too close to their bedroom. Unfortunately, everything was tight in the small space.

"What are you doing?" Eleanor narrowed her eyes. "I said I was going to work on the bed area. You can figure out how you're going to set up your workbench once I'm done. I'll need more than walking space if I need to be alone."

"But with the shop area you want up front, there's hardly enough for the anvil and fire. I need to have a larger area to experiment with the materials we collect. Testing the properties can sometimes get messy."

"I know how much you care about the forge, but I have some ideas too." She crossed her arms and looked to the ground. "You need to trust me."

"How much room do you need for the bed?" Sindrick tried to hold his ground, but a pain thumped in his chest. "Building a new forge is going to be hard without worrying about condensing everything right away. Once it gets going, we can move things around again."

"I suppose you'll do what you want." She sighed and shoved past him to build the frame for their bed. "Get the fire burning. It's getting cold in here."

Sindrick left the marking sticks on the ground and carefully took out the fire stones from their bag. A few logs remained in the opening for the fireplace. He made sure the ventilation was working and threw his creation in. It ignited instantly.

He turned to see Eleanor had hung some pieces of the canvas tent to create walls for the bedroom. It was near the place he marked off. He smiled to himself but did not feel relieved that she listened to his advice about the space.

Eleanor stayed behind the canvas the rest of the afternoon while he finished setting up his anvil and forge. He created more shelves with the ropes and unpacked his tools to be ready for the long days ahead.

"I have our bed area done," Eleanor called out. "Would you care to join me?"

Sindrick realized he was staring at the flames again and blinked to adjust his eyes to the rest of the dark room. Eleanor stood with one of the blankets wrapped loosely around her. The spark in her eyes was more dazzling than the idea of a renewable fire.

"Yes, I'd like to see it," Sindrick said. "I'm sorry about earlier."

"Everything's already forgotten," she said and slipped behind the canvas.

Sindrick followed her around to their new bedroom. He let out a small gasp of wonder from the moonlight illuminating the display. Eleanor had suspended the bed off the floor using some knotwork beyond his skill, and she managed to create a place for their clothes in a unique wardrobe of rope and fabric.

"It will hold both of us." Eleanor patted the spot next to her. "I know your work is important to you, so I wanted to give you as much space as possible to study the elements. But I also need a place to get away as well. I hope you like it."

"It's almost as magical as you are," he said and kissed her hand. "This must have taken a while. Were you able to rest like you wanted?"

"There will be time to rest later," she said as Sindrick climbed under the covers. "Awake or asleep, any moment we share is exactly where I want to be. We can build a forge in our hearts burning forever."

93

"Such a flame would be greater than any metal I could fashion. Tomorrow we can finish setting up, and soon we will have our own shop."

"That's not what I meant." Eleanor sighed and rolled over. "I should probably sleep. I'm more tired than I thought and want to hunt for some gems in the morning."

Sindrick rubbed her back, but she didn't respond. His adrenaline would not allow him to rest anytime soon. He wondered if he could sneak out and craft his work station.

Instead, he decided to watch the woman sleeping next to him. The moonlight and glow from the forge reflected softly across her cheek. He wanted to keep her image in his mind and never forget the girl with the raven hair and emerald eyes again.

But he couldn't shake the fear of her figuring out he wasn't the man she thought he was. He was simply an apprentice trying to be greater than his master.

9

The ice crystals in the air refracted the morning sun, creating a halo of colors around it. Sindrick never imagined how spectacular the landscape was in the north until he gazed across the open water. The hidden trail down the cliff's side only gave enough room for one to squeeze through at a time. It wound behind walls and through cramped tunnels.

Sindrick couldn't help but admire the rocks on their trek. The metal elements mixed within the cliff were more durable than anything he had fashioned. It had lasted for centuries in the same state, even with the waves pounding against it.

"Careful," Sindrick called back to Eleanor, who was following behind him. "The waves are kicking up a lot of moisture in the air.

The rocks aren't slick, but in these conditions, that could change fast."

"I'm surprised this whole area isn't coated in ice," Eleanor said and wrapped her fur cape tighter. "Are these stones heated from something?"

Sindrick stopped and stared at one of the rocks beside him. He pressed his cheek to it. A small vibration of electric energy tingled his skin.

"I'd like to study this more," he said and turned to Eleanor. Her displeasure was apparent. "That is, once we reach the bottom."

"I am ready to get out of the wind. You said there were caves down here. How much farther is it?"

"It shouldn't be long," Sindrick guessed. "Probably around the next few turns."

They continued until the path split into multiple directions. Most of them led to the shoreline. Sindrick decided to take one extending across the ridge. It soon turned sharply to a cave in the side of the cliff with enough room for both of them to enter side by side.

After they stooped down through the opening, the hidden entrance revealed a larger cavern. The path wove through an open area until it dropped off steeply to the sea. The way the rocks formed around the water created a pond with a mirrored surface. It looked to be replenished from an underground reservoir and spilled out to the sea.

"I can see a way to get down," Sindrick said and grabbed Eleanor's hand.

The salt and earth mixed into a fresh scent. Unlike the shores he remembered, there was no stench of rotting fish. The water hardly graced itself upon the rocks. . . rocks he had never seen before.

The cut of the minerals amplified the streams of light coming in from the opening. Along the wall, quartz of every size and color reflected into Sindrick's eyes. He ran a hand across one taller than himself. Each crystal contained a multitude of attributes. Some were clear enough to be used as a magnifying lens to look closer at the properties of the ones he would study.

"This is incredible," he said and picked up a dislodged chunk the size of his fist. "Do you have any idea what these can do? There's almost too much for me to understand."

"I've seen ones smaller than this going for amounts we couldn't begin to count." Eleanor twirled around the room.

"We wouldn't need anything else." Sindrick smiled and ran his fingers through his hair. "We need to keep this place a secret. I know some people who would want to raid its treasures."

"You're thinking of Crowell, aren't you?" Eleanor raised her eyebrow. "You shouldn't worry about him. He's getting off land for a while."

"How do you know he's leaving?" Jealousy fought at Sindrick's mind. "Did you run into him before we left Virfell?"

"The barkeep mentioned it." She looked away to the cove below the edge of the cliff. "Look at this!" She grabbed his hand to pull him closer. "There's enough room to fit an entire ship. I'm surprised no one has stashed one here."

"Not many travel this way. At least, not to stay." Sindrick tapped his foot on the ground. "It is a minor stop in their final passing. I'm not sure if I told you why my father ventured to the frozen hills."

"You mentioned that he left after your mother's death. I'm sorry for what happened."

"It's not that. . . I don't think my father believed she actually died." Sindrick dropped Eleanor's hand to pick up another crystal and turned it over. "Something happened to his mind. He said my mother spoke to him, and she wanted him to join her."

98

"Some people believe our loved ones are never truly gone."

"It's not the same as those tales. A force outside of his own guided him. He wandered alone at night in the streets of Virfell. I sometimes followed him. He kept ranting about a darkness being lost and recovered. After weeks of those remarks and speaking of dead trees, he suddenly changed back. He was normal and happy. At least, I thought so. It wasn't long until he took the journey to the frozen hills. Nothing survives there."

"I know the legends," Eleanor said and put her hand on his arm. "I grew up in this area, don't you remember? Any creature able to endure the harsh environment would not be a kind one. My ancestors also traveled to the far northern hills at the end of their lives."

"I'm not so sure I could do it." Sindrick slipped some of the crystals into his bag. "I'd be too afraid of the unknown horrors. I know it's tradition, but I'd rather die in a familiar place."

"As long as you keep me with you, it will always be a familiar place." Eleanor gave him a quick kiss on the cheek. "Of course, it would be nice to get our shop going before we get too old. Will you be able to use some of these stones for your alchemy testing? I need you to unlock my amulet soon."

"I'll figure it out with the right tools and time." As he spoke, his breath escaped in frost, and a chill pierced through the layers of fur around him.

"What's happening?" Eleanor pulled him closer. "I can't feel my face anymore."

"It didn't look like it would storm today." Sindrick shivered from the sudden temperature drop. "Maybe there's a breeze coming off the sea. It's early in the day, and the sun has yet to heat the ground. It should warm up again."

"Did you bring any of your fire stones with you?"

"No. I didn't think we'd need them. I'm not sure if there's enough ventilation in here anyway."

"Let's go home." Eleanor walked toward the cave's opening. "Grab what you need, and we can come back later."

"How am I supposed to choose out of all this?" Sindrick muttered to himself. His eyes were wide from the cacophony of possibilities around them. "You can head back if you want. I'll catch up."

"You need to remember who it is you brought with you."

"What?" Sindrick turned to see Eleanor grasp something under her cloak. Her eyes had a dark aura in them as she glared at him.

"Nevermind," she said sharply. "I'm leaving."

Eleanor slipped out of the cavern before he could respond.

Sindrick stood in shock from the cold and the sudden change in her tone. He opened the bag and shoved as many rocks into it as he could. It was likely he grabbed multiple ones with the same abilities and not any unique gems. He regretfully shouldered the bag and followed the trail back to their home.

"It's warmer out now," Sindrick said, opening the door. "We should've stayed longer down there. I grabbed a few stones so I could hurry back to you."

He waited for Eleanor's response, but the building remained silent.

"Are you home?" he called out as a sense of panic caused his stomach to turn. "Eleanor?"

He rushed inside and pulled back the canvas to their bedroom.

The room went completely dark except for a strange light around Eleanor. She sat with her legs crossed and hands clutched around the amulet. Her head was down, but Sindrick thought there were black trails of smoke coming from her eyes.

Across her skin, words had been tattooed that were never there before. They crawled through her skin, growing larger and

101

smaller. New ones formed in a burnt pattern Sindrick could almost smell.

Eleanor's lips moved as if she were speaking, but no sound escaped. The entire room was engulfed in silence, making Sindrick wonder if he had lost his hearing. Whatever she communicated with went beyond the normal senses.

The haze in the air caused Sindrick to rub his eyes. At once, he was staring into their regular bedroom. Eleanor slept quietly in the bed as if nothing happened. She moaned at him and turned over, covering her head in the blankets.

"Sorry," Sindrick whispered and carefully closed the canvas door.

He peeked back inside. Her arms no longer had any markings on them as he witnessed, or thought he'd seen.

Sindrick exhaled slowly after holding his breath during the vision.

"I must be exhausted," he said to himself. "I need to refocus my sanity."

He tried to set the bag of stones near his anvil quietly, but the rocks clanged against one another. There wouldn't be a way for him to forge anything, and he needed to create a workspace for studying the materials properly.

After placing another log on the fire, he started to separate the crystals on the floor. Until Eleanor woke, there would not be much he could do. And he feared what he would see if he tried to check on her again.

"How long was I out?" Eleanor asked as Sindrick examined the stones under his make-shift magnifying lens.

He was right about what he grabbed. Most of them were from the same area and possessed similar abilities. There was one promising enough to work for his renewable fire theory, but it would need proper testing.

"You slept most of the day," Sindrick said. "The sun is still up, but I wasn't keeping track of time."

He stood up to stretch from crawling on the ground so he could study the stones. A table or desk would have been ideal. His stomach grumbled, and he took a sip of the water they brought with them.

"We need to get a plan together for how we're going to get more food," he said and offered the bottle to Eleanor. "The villagers here might not trade for raw gems. I don't want you to keep spending your fortune."

"You can make them things." Eleanor finished off the water and set the empty bottle on one of the shelves.

"It's not so easy." Sindrick sighed and looked around the room.

With the right materials, it would take at least a week to get some items crafted to sell. And he didn't have a good carrier metal for the gems. It would take more searching in the cave.

"You'll figure something out," she said and secured her gloves. "We need to get the storefront set up first anyway."

"I can go into the market and see if I could work for the supplies."

"Don't worry about what we need," Eleanor said and gave him an abrupt kiss. "I need you focused on what I want—this shop. Can you get things running soon?"

"I'll bang out a few things." Sindrick smiled. "I didn't want to disturb your rest earlier. It shouldn't take me long."

"Good." She pulled a few more layers of fur over her. "I may be out for a while. Once you set it up, I'd like you to examine this."

She handed him the amulet with the strange black stone. It was warm from being close to Eleanor's skin but gave Sindrick a chill within his soul.

"Keep it near you," she said with a stern look. "Don't let anyone else know you have it. I can't read rocks like you do, but I know it's important."

"It is a mystery," Sindrick said, peering into the void of the gem. "I will let you know what I find out about it."

"That's why you're so amazing." Eleanor gave him a long hug before she turned to exit. "You shouldn't worry yourself over me. I can take care of myself. I've had to most of my life, and it's not like we're married." Her last remark was almost inaudible as she slipped into the open air.

"I'm here to help you—" Sindrick started to say, but Eleanor closed the door on him.

He tossed the stone in the air and caught it quickly. Its weight felt less dense than a standard gem, like it was hollow inside. But gazing into it, the material's solid core seemed to be staring back.

"I need to examine you properly," he said aloud and placed the rock into the pouch hanging off his belt. "After I get this place straightened up."

With Eleanor gone, he set to work hammering out the nails and tools he needed to craft a table. That part was easy. Searching through the debris they tossed out for anything salvageable proved to be a tedious task.

The sun grew weary on the horizon while Sindrick dug through the salt-crusted materials. After a few bouts of swearing and tying together various scraps of wood, he had a stable place to set his work.

He managed to find a few sturdy poles to create a base for a stool. Weaving extra rope between them provided a comfortable seat. With his newly collected crystals sectioned in their proper spot and the chair beneath him, he took out the amulet and placed it at the center of the table.

The gem's listless wonder continued to hide its secrets from him.

"Where did you come from?" he whispered.

He put his arms on the table and rested his chin on them. His eyelids became heavy as exhaustion overtook his will to study. The warmth of the forge next to him lulled him into a dreamless state where darkness covered everything, like the clouds covering the stars outside.

10

A banging on the door shook Sindrick awake. His eyes burned from the light spilling in from outside. He went to rub them and found he was clutching the amulet in his palm.

The knocking continued, and he dropped the stone into his pouch. His fingers ached from gripping it so tightly.

"Eleanor? Are you back already?" He called out in a groggy voice. "The door should be unlocked."

"Hope you don't mind us barging in," Dan said, doing exactly that.

He stepped in quickly with his new wife close behind. Rena looked around the place with a furrowed brow.

"Looks like you need to do quite a lot of work here," she said. "It does look better on the inside than the mess outside."

"Thanks," Sindrick said sarcastically and stood to show off his handiwork. "Once we get the shop set up, I'll get everything else fixed. How did you find me anyway? I don't recall Crowell knowing where I went. Is he okay?"

"I never liked him, but I think he's gone completely mad," Rena said. "I hope he didn't try hurting you. He kept going on like a lunatic about—"

"He's his usual self," Dan interrupted. "Maybe a little crazier and over-eager to share every detail of your trip together. We found the previous host for you two, Tompkins. He said he helped you buy this place. Well. . . he said the woman you were with gave him a price he couldn't turn down." He led Rena over to the stool. "May we?"

Sindrick nodded, and Rena eased herself onto the newly crafted chair.

"You didn't see Eleanor in town while you were there, did you?" Sindrick looked out the window, hoping she wouldn't come in and see the unannounced visitors.

"We figured she was with you," Rena said and looked to Dan, who kept his head down. "The barkeep said you left with her and mentioned traveling to the north. It had the rest of the town talking about it. Is everything okay with you two? She said she knew your family growing up, but Jack said he had some suspicions about her."

"Everything is fine." Sindrick crossed his arms. "Jack is wary of anyone new, especially if it's someone I like to be around. Dan, you probably remember when Crowell first came to town. I had to practically beg him to let me use his chemicals again for my alchemy." He leaned against the wall. "I hope you two don't think Eleanor is bad for me. She's the one who helped me get this place set up and went out to get us more supplies. There's no need to worry about me."

"I'm sure it's our own fears and nothing to be concerned about." Rena nudged Dan. "Someone else might be missing you too."

"It's true, and you know I'll support your choices," Dan said. "You've always been full of wild ideas, but somehow they work."

"I'm glad someone has faith in me." Sindrick sighed. "By the way, have you heard anything about her family? She's so secretive, and I can't remember them."

"They were the soldier-of-fortune type," Dan said, rubbing Rena's back. "Her father was always seeking a better place to sell their wares. And like most people in our village, they moved away with the promise of richer gain. I vaguely remember meeting them. Their shop was always warm, and her mother gave us gingerbread when we came through."

"Now we know why you don't remember what they sold. All you remember is the sweets." Sindrick poked Dan's stomach and laughed.

"So, do you really like Eleanor?" Dan asked.

"I couldn't be happier." The question made him uneasy. "You of all people should know what it feels like to find the right one. I thought you were on my side."

"We are," Dan said, placing his hands together to apologize. "Please don't take what I said the wrong way. I do have some good news—well, some good, some bad."

"What's the bad news?"

"After we talked with Crowell, he said he was going to leave again."

"That's nothing new," Sindrick scoffed. "You had me worried."

"It's not one of the brothels he usually visits." Dan's wife nudged him in the ribs, and he cleared his throat. "I mean, his. . . familiar ports. Anyway, he kept raving about the beast he was convinced followed him, which is part of the reason why we wanted to check on you."

"Honestly, I didn't see anything of the creature he described, but he looked more terrified than the night before your wedding." Sindrick moved a couple of empty boxes over so they could sit together. "The look in his eyes convinced me to return to Virfell without him."

"We're more worried about why he's leaving," Rena said and held her stomach. "He said he had found something out about the troll king, Gostav. His ship was spotted near Virfell. You know how he goes on about the untraceable ship."

"Crowell's not going after him, is he?"

Rena glanced at Dan, and he nodded.

"Idiot!" Sindrick stood back up. "I know he wants to be the first to take out the scourge, but there's always more than one ship. It would be suicide."

"He may have a chance at defeating Gostav this time," Dan held up his bandaged finger and pointed at it with his good hand. "My guess is that he's going to work on controlling the creatures he summons from the sea's abyss. The birds were a test."

"Magic gives me the chills," Rena chimed in. "Using any type of power for your own end always leads to madness. You can't expect to bend someone's mind without losing part of yours. My grandfather told me as much."

111

"I'd agree with your grandfather." Sindrick paced anxiously around the room. "Crowell's been acting differently ever since his last journey. The dark spells keep bringing more destruction. Perhaps I could create an item to counter their sway on his mind."

"I grew up hearing stories of fae using true magic," Rena said. "Some of the refugees in Northeal were rumored to trade with them."

"Yeah, but Crowell said he learned his spells from Raikrune, further south," Dan interjected. "He probably has a harem down there too." Rena elbowed him again. "Sorry, but it's Crowell, wouldn't surprise me."

"Me neither." Sindrick shook his head. "Anyway, you said you had good news too?"

"Yes, we do," Dan stood up, but Rena stepped in front of him.

"I want to tell him," she said with a glowing smile. "We're having a baby soon."

"What? Already?" Sindrick's joy took him by surprise. "I didn't know they could determine it so fast."

"We may have known for a while." Dan looked around the room. "Which is why the wedding was moved up. You know how people are in our village."

"Nothing like the controversy of a baby out of wedlock to be the talk of the town. Your parents would be the worst about it too."

"We snuck away after the party to find out for certain," Dan said and helped Rena sit back down. "We told my parents that we found a special healer who gave us the news sooner than a normal one."

"Smart move." Sindrick tapped the side of his nose. "I wondered why you left without telling anyone where you were going. Hopefully, you had some time to yourselves."

"We did," Rena said with a grin. Her face became more serious, and she motioned for him to sit. "I hope it's not too forward to ask, would you keep the time I became pregnant a secret from Eleanor? We don't want many people to know about it happening before the ceremony, and we've known you longer."

"You know I can keep a secret." Sindrick didn't like the idea of keeping anything from Eleanor, but at the same time, she withheld a lot from him. "You should let her know of your pregnancy, at least."

"You do hide a lot of secrets, don't you?" Dan asked. "Ever since we were young, you were the one everyone would go to without fear of gossip. Jack used to say that you preferred talking

113

to stones over people, which is likely why your skills with crafting metal are more impressive than you give yourself credit. I've always wondered how you do it."

"It's difficult to explain."

Dan shrugged and leaned down to sit when the door burst open. He toppled onto the floor. Sindrick couldn't help but laugh at the sight with Eleanor's look of confusion and brandished dagger.

"Welcome back," he said to her as she walked in. "I guess Tompkins told these two where we were hiding."

"There were horses outside, and I thought it could be trouble," Eleanor said and tucked the knife back into her belt. "I would've cleaned up the place if I knew friends were coming over. It's Dan and Rena, right?"

"That's us," Dan said and steadied himself against the wall.

"Sorry for rushing in. Would you care for anything to drink? I picked up some rum in town."

Sindrick looked at Rena, who gave an awkward smile.

"We're fine, thank you." Dan cleared his throat. "I was hoping you'd be here. You both left in such a hurry before we were able to give you the good news. My wife is pregnant."

The Salty Eleanor

"What wonderful news!" Eleanor said and hugged Rena. "I thought you looked different from when I saw you last. Sindrick, can you grab the bag outside? It's beside the door."

Sindrick nodded and rushed out at her request.

The sunlight caused him to blink. It was a good day for traveling as the air had a deceptive warmth to it. It was the first cloudless day since they moved up north.

"You two should stay and have a meal with us," Sindrick said when he returned.

Eleanor shot him a glare while holding out her hand. She snatched the bag and dug through it.

"There should be enough here for four," she said without looking back up.

Sindrick helped her sort the items. "I'm sure we could make room if you needed to stay for the night as well. It will be too late to make the journey back to Virfell at this hour."

"You probably don't want to stay long," Eleanor said. "I was informed the pass is going to be frozen over soon."

"We hadn't planned on visiting more than today," Dan said. "Although, there is something I thought would be fun to do while we're up here. Tompkins said this place was close to the sea. How much of a walk is it?"

"It's over the next ridge," Sindrick said. "On a good day, you can almost hear—"

"We should show you," Eleanor interrupted. "If you'd like to get your horses ready, Sindrick and I will pack a small snack and get the rest of this organized."

"I would like that very much," Rena said and grabbed Dan's hand, who looked like he wanted to protest. "We'll wait outside for you."

Eleanor gave a cheerful smile while they left. As soon as the door closed, she wrapped her arms around Sindrick and pulled him close.

"What are they doing up here?" she whispered harshly. "No one was supposed to know about this place, and they could've sent a message through a courier to let us know about the pregnancy."

"Crowell got them stirred up, and they wanted to make sure we were safe. Everyone talks in Virfell."

"They weren't looking for anything else, were they?" She quickly let him go and walked over to the table. "It looks like you've been busy. Did you figure out anything with the amulet? Where is it?"

She scattered the piles of rocks around the desk.

"I have it with me," Sindrick said, grabbing her arm before she destroyed the rest of his organized work.

"Sorry, I shouldn't have left the jewel." She held her hand out and gave him a look he couldn't resist. "May I have it back?"

Sindrick pulled the necklace out of his pouch. "I wasn't able to unlock its abilities yet, but I'm sure I can with enough study."

"Yes, you will." Eleanor fashioned it around her neck and smiled. "I'll get the food prepared if you want to make sure the others are ready to go. It's the perfect day for a picnic."

11

It took them longer than usual to reach the cliffs overlooking the sea. Sindrick decided to lead his friends away from the passage to the secret cove, hoping to keep it hidden. The warmth from the sun created soft spots of mud along the path. Eleanor made a few comments about slowing down for Rena, but Sindrick knew she didn't like getting her clothes or boots dirty.

"I never imagined anything like this from what Tompkins said of the view," Rena said as she spread out a blanket near the edge. "This place is beautiful. We may need to move our home closer to the north."

"No," Eleanor blurted out. "It would be harsh for a newborn in the winter, and it's far too secluded for any healers to help with your pregnancy."

The Salty Eleanor

"It would be better for us to remain in Virfell," Dan agreed. "If the fate's allow, we will have a healthy number of children. This is the first of many."

"I wish the best for your family," Sindrick said and reclined with the others. "It would be nice to have some familiar faces up here, but it does get cut off from the rest of the world when the frost comes. I'm hoping the people here will have an interest in alchemy as well as blacksmithing."

"What are you going to do up here?" Rena asked Eleanor.

"We'll be opening a shop at the front." Eleanor squeezed Sindrick's hand. "I'll run the business and help with ideas. I know Sindrick can craft more than tools and weapons. I bet he could create a form of full armor from a wristband."

"Come to think of it, it wouldn't be too hard," Sindrick said, rubbing his chin. "I would also like to find a mineral allowing us to sleep less. I find it unnecessary."

"I imagined you already figured out that secret," Dan said with a laugh. "You've always been working nonstop on your next project, or multiple at once. Don't worry, Eleanor. I'm sure he's not as bad anymore."

"It's okay if he is," she said and tore off a hunk of bread to share. "I like it about him. He's very focused on what he is doing, even if it doesn't make sense to the rest of us."

"My methods are carefully planned." Sindrick took a bite and looked across the waves.

Deep beneath their surface rested an entire world of metals and rocks waiting to be discovered. The cave he found provided a small glimpse of what the waters could produce. During the falling tide, he could venture closer if he created something to keep him safe from the elements.

"Something's wrong," Rena said and went into a fit of coughs. "I'm not—"

She leaned forward, covering her mouth with a rag while she continued to cough. Her skin turned pale as she started to shake.

Dan picked her up in both arms. The look in his eyes spoke what he wanted to say. They needed to get back to the warmth of the home.

"Grab what you can," Sindrick told Eleanor. "I'll get them back."

Eleanor grabbed onto his hand and pulled herself up. "It can be replaced. Let's go."

They helped Rena onto the horse, and Dan climbed on behind to keep her secure. A cold breeze caused them to shiver as the light of the sun vanished behind the gathering clouds. With a flick of the reigns, they hurried down the path to the forge.

"Sorry to ruin our time together," Rena said when they sat her near the fireplace.

Sindrick made sure the logs were burning steadily and searched the crystals on the workbench. He discovered the ones needed to make warmth without flame or smoke, but it would take a few more adjustments to work correctly.

"I don't know if it was the cold or something we ate on the way up," Rena continued as Dan rubbed her back. "We were going to find a room in the village, but it might be best to take your offer on staying tonight."

"You are more than welcome here," Sindrick said, brushing Rena's hair back.

"Don't feel bad about what happened," Eleanor said and took a swig of rum. "Everyone gets sick when they're pregnant."

"Are you sure you're okay?" Dan asked. "I can get you whatever you like."

"I could use some more water," Rena said. "I should've said something before we walked up the hill. I was so thirsty but didn't want to be impolite."

Eleanor took Dan's place by her side while he left to fill up a mug. "I'm guessing it was the oncoming cold snap. I sensed it in the air too." She stood up and looked out the window. "You'll want to leave early to travel in the middle of the day. Getting caught out there with the sun going down wouldn't be wise."

Rena nodded. The color had returned to her cheeks. Whatever happened earlier had passed.

Eleanor drank more from her bottle and walked closer to Sindrick.

"Can I talk with you outside?" she whispered.

"It's a little cold out there, can it wait?"

Sindrick tapped the rocks he was holding and looked at the couple by the fireplace. He wanted to remain near them in case anything happened again.

Eleanor held his arm gently. "Please. It's important."

The urgency in her voice made Sindrick sigh. He put the stones into his pouch to study later and followed Eleanor to the door.

"We'll need to be quick," he said. "I want to make sure the fire stays warm for our guests. I have an idea for an alternative, but it will take time to perfect."

"You really have too many projects going at once."

Eleanor laughed while they headed into the brisk air. Even with the layers of fur covering him, the wind managed to pierce through and chill Sindrick's bones. He placed his hands under his armpits to keep his core warm.

"I can't live like this," Eleanor said as her joyful composure turned to sorrow. "I don't know if we are going to stay together or if this is a momentary thing. You keep saying you want to be with me. But then you want me to leave so you can work, or you want to be with your friends instead of me. What do you want?"

"I want to be with you." Sindrick grasped her hands in his. They were chilled, and he tried to warm them with his own. "I'm sorry if I seemed hesitant about us moving in together. It's not something people do here. But no matter where we are or what happens, I want you with me. Once we get things going with the forge and shop, we can share more time with each other."

"So, will you marry me?" She looked deep into his eyes.

Sindrick's mind fell into their celestial gaze. He tried to hide his surprise and the rush of blood pounding from his chest. His knees weakened, causing him to stumble toward her.

"Yes!" The response came out before he understood what he was saying. He hardly knew anything about the woman before him, yet she was everything he could imagine.

Eleanor's lips seemed fuller as she closed her eyes to kiss him. The frozen air almost locked their flesh together. Her cheeks felt warm against his freezing nose as they escaped the shell of their bodies in their mind, floating into the stars beaming down on the crisp night. They shone above them in harmony with their love. Everything was perfect.

"We should travel back with Dan and Rena tomorrow," Eleanor said, wrapping her arms around him. "It would be nice to be married in Virfell with your friends around us. We'll return here to build our life together after the celebration."

Sindrick nodded as he shivered from the cold and anticipation.

"Your parents won't mind that I didn't ask for their blessing, will they?" he asked.

"My parents don't know I'm here." She squeezed his hand and quickly slipped inside to the warmth of the fire.

The Salty Eleanor

Sindrick remained in the doorway. His assumptions about Eleanor became wrapped in more mystery. She was an indistinguishable enigma in the formation of elements. But whatever pattern it was, she had agreed to be with him forever. . . or he had accepted her proposal. However it happened, nothing would be able to hinder their love.

12

Sindrick latched the two rocks together, and they instantly warmed the room. He had finished crafting them on the journey back to Virfell. Dan and Rena agreed to let him and Eleanor stay in the new addition to their home. It would eventually be a nursery, but it didn't have the proper insulation finished.

"This should keep us warm and would make a nice gift for the new family," Sindrick said and rubbed his hands over the stones.

"Can we talk about the wedding?" Eleanor asked, wrapping her arms around his waist. "You didn't tell your friends about our marriage on the way back. We need to spread the word so we can be together sooner."

"I figured it would take some time to plan everything." Sindrick's throat dried up. "Are you saying you want to get married right now?"

"Yes." Eleanor twirled him around and smiled. "It won't take much time to prepare. We should have the ceremony after the next night."

"I'm worried the townsfolk might get suspicious and not show up."

"You need to stop concerning yourself over your friends. I'm sure they could use something new to talk about, and I've witnessed stranger things than a quick ceremony. On one of my journeys, I met a human who was married to an elf. They tried to hide it, but I could see their love for each other. The way they moved together was beautiful."

"I honestly can't come up with a reason why we shouldn't be married immediately," Sindrick said, but a million thoughts swarmed his mind. "I guess rumors shouldn't hurt our business."

"Do you ever think about my feelings?" She pouted and crossed her arms.

"I didn't mean it that way. I'm sorry." He reached out to her, but she backed away. "So, you only need a day to get everything ready?"

"Probably less, but for the sake of this town, it will take a few more resources."

Sindrick tried to smile in agreement. His concern made it look more like a grimace.

"I should get to work," Eleanor said. "Don't wait up for me. I'll be busy getting the ceremony lined up, so you can be the one to let your friends know about it."

"Dan and Rena went on about how tired they were from the journey. They may be asleep already."

"You have all day tomorrow to explain it to them," Eleanor said and gave him a quick kiss before departing.

"Be cautious, and take my love with you," Sindrick called out.

He took a deep breath. His way with words needed to improve, but he hoped Eleanor understood his mumbling. He needed a drink.

After carefully unlatching the warming stones, he grabbed a few coins Eleanor left behind and headed toward the tavern.

"Crowell's going to kill you when he gets back," Jack said when Sindrick told him about the wedding.

He had been in his usual spot at the bar, sniffing one of his homebrews and trying to convince the barkeep to buy a supply.

Sindrick had to admit it tasted better than others being sold at the tavern. He helped play it up to the barkeep until the man finally agreed to purchase a small portion to test on the patrons.

"It wasn't my plan to get married so quick," Sindrick said, letting Jack pour him another cup of his brew. "Thank you for wanting to help with the drinks. You've created something rather fine, for once. I'll have to get the recipe to use for some experiments."

"The secret is in its simplicity." Jack held the jug up like a trophy. "It's refreshing and unsuspectingly strong. Don't take it at face value, or it will bite your head clean off. . . kind of like Eleanor."

"What do you mean?" Sindrick clenched his fist and reeled back.

"I'm messing with you." Jack laughed. "From what I've heard, she is quite the taskmaster. You'll have your hands full. Don't say I didn't warn you."

"She knows what she wants and gets it. Dan and Rena seem to like her, but I haven't told them about the wedding yet. They have enough on their mind with the new baby." He tapped the cup and took a small sip to calm his nerves.

"I realized something terrible!" Jack grabbed Sindrick's shoulder. "Kate has already been pressuring me about getting her family's blessing because of their baby. Can you imagine what she'll do once she finds out you're getting married before us? You want me to die a miserable man, don't you?"

"You know me too well," Sindrick teased. "I figured you could use a bit of a push to get married and join us old couples."

"Well, I guess it won't be half as bad when Crowell finds out. You better drink heavily while you can." Jack poured himself another glass and topped off Sindrick's. "Can you get one of those messenger ships out to him?"

"I thought about it, but you know how he is on his hunts."

Jack nodded and motioned for him to drink.

The two threw back another round together, finishing off the homebrew. The frown on Jack's face caused Sindrick to slap his coins down on the bar. A couple more bottles of the tavern's darkest lager slid in front of them.

"It's probably for the best you didn't," Jack said and eyed the drink. "If he truly is hunting down trolls, especially Gostav, another ship could give away his position."

"Sometimes I wonder why we keep warring with them." It became harder for Sindrick to formulate words in his state. "I thought they killed the troll king already. Isn't Gostav his son?"

"He killed his father so he could be king." Jack stood up and steadied himself on a chair. "I bet Crowell has it lodged in his head that if he defeats Gostav, he'll be the greatest warrior on the seas. But it's impossible to know what the captain's motives are."

"I'm surprised he agreed to help me find a place in the north. You'd think he'd stick around longer to get the sword I promised him. Maybe he did go crazy with his summoning spells."

"You'd be the one to know crazy, getting married so soon." Jack nudged Sindrick. "I'm surprised she went for you and not. . . nevermind."

"What?" Sindrick raised his eyebrow. "You were going to say Crowell, weren't you?"

Jack shrugged and hid his face while drinking from his mug.

"Apart from Dan, you've known me the longest," Sindrick said and sat back. "I've been there for you during the multiple times you and Kate have split and then gotten back together. I'm reserved in most aspects of my life, but I know what I'm doing with Eleanor. She believes in my abilities and wants to see me draw out the powers of the elements."

"I've helped you too." Jack slumped in his chair. "Remember all the mixtures we talked about and the chemicals I gave you to test? I see you as a true blacksmith who can forge items beyond the natural world."

"I think your brew is speaking," Sindrick said and slapped Jack on the back. "You're getting dangerously close to giving me a proper compliment. We've usually had more drinks before such talk."

"Fair point." He pounded his chest and let out a belch. "Maybe this stuff shouldn't be sold. It's too strong for anyone, even me."

"Can you imagine what it would do to Crowell?"

Jack lifted his empty cup to Sindrick. "The good news is you won't have to worry about him taking you on the night ride."

"I need my fingers for forging."

"True enough." Jack nodded to the barkeep, and he got them another bottle. "Speaking of missing limbs, we should talk to Dan. He'll throw one of his hissy fits if he's the last to know."

"But he and his wife are sleeping." Sindrick placed a finger to his lips, already feeling the numbness from the intense alcohol. "We can't be loud around someone pregnant. Maybe? I don't know. Have you been around babies much?"

"You're the biggest one I've met." Jack punched Sindrick's arm and stumbled off the chair.

They snuck out into the night and helped each other walk toward Dan's home.

Jack grabbed a handful of rocks outside of the house. He threw them one by one at the shuttered window until Dan opened up. One nearly missed his head as their trajectory grew progressively worse.

"What are you doing out there?" Dan called out in a hushed voice. "It's the middle of the night."

"He's getting married," Jack said and jabbed a finger into Sindrick's chest.

Sindrick stumbled back from the unexpected gesture. His head reeled from the additional alcohol they imbibed on the way to the house. He bent down to steady himself from emptying his churning stomach.

"Who's getting married?" Dan asked, leaning out the window. "Is Kate finally making an honest man out of you?"

"No, not me." Jack pushed Sindrick forward.

"Eleanor asked me—I mean, I'm getting married in a couple of days," Sindrick said and hiccuped. "Or is it a day and a half? After the next night is the celebration in the morning."

Dan quickly shut the window and rushed out the front door to meet them.

"Why didn't you tell me before?" he asked and helped Sindrick up the steps to the porch. "Did you know about this before we came to see you?"

"It happened fast. She wants us to get married right away so we can go back up north."

"Marriage is a commitment. It's not to be taken lightly." Dan grabbed both of Sindrick's arms. "Does this mean you remembered growing up with her? It seems risky to be with someone you just met."

"My childhood is forgotten." Sindrick shrugged him off. "We have our whole lives to catch up on what we missed. You guys are supposed to be excited for me."

"I'd expect Crowell to do something like this, not you." Dan folded his arms and sat down hard on a wicker chair. "Does he know?"

"We wouldn't be here if he did," Jack said. "I bet he'd take Sindrick out for the whole day on his ship. Probably end up losing more than a finger."

Dan narrowed his eyes, and Sindrick couldn't help but laugh at the two.

"Keep it down," Dan whispered. "Rena's asleep and pregnant. You probably want to live to see your wedding day. We will celebrate tomorrow night."

"At least have a drink with us to sample Jack's new brew," Sindrick said. "We can go to the room you have me staying in. Eleanor went out to get supplies for the wedding. And I should show you what I discovered. Wait, it's a gift. Forget about what I said."

Sindrick covered Dan's eyes before he realized his foolishness.

"Come on," Dan said and batted Sindrick's hand away. "I guess if Jack made something you actually like, it must be amazing."

Sindrick had to hold his breath to keep from laughing as they tiptoed around the house. The new addition hadn't been connected to the rest of the home yet. It was a perfect resting place before the wedding, and a secluded spot to drink more bottles of Jack's latest concoction.

135

Matthew E. Nordin

13

Sunlight burned in Sindrick's eyes as the door flung open. He tried to shut them tighter and ignore the stomping of feet echoing off the wooden floor. Each step grew more painful with his amplifying headache.

"Hello?" he managed to mutter and rolled over in the bed.

"Oh good, you're up." Eleanor's voice gave him peace, but he struggled to open his eyes. "I have something for you."

"I hope it convinces me never to drink anything Jack makes again." Sindrick sat up and rubbed his head. "Were you out all night?"

"No, I returned a while ago and helped you into bed. You were passed out on the floor."

She sat next to him and handed him a wooden mug. The warm liquid inside soothed his cramped fingers. All of his joints ached.

"Drink up," she said and helped him lift it to his lips. "It will make you more alert. We have much to do today."

Sindrick took a sip of the sweetened tea. Hints of strawberry and mint warmed his tongue and throat.

After a few more gulps, the pounding in his head subsided.

"Thank you," he said and stretched his back. "I told Jack and Dan about the wedding. They were surprised."

"I'll make sure they show up," Eleanor said and ruffled his hair. "I need you to get a large cart for us to bring everything to our northern shop. Once the ceremony is over, we will need to depart immediately before the pass freezes over."

"I can help with more of the wedding." Sindrick took another drink. "You don't have to set up everything by yourself."

"I'll manage. You should spend the day with your friends. Once we are married and start our life together at the new forge, we won't be back for quite some time. Your friends need to understand that and respect our solitude."

"If the only time I ever have is with you, I will be content."

"Good." Eleanor smiled. "Now turn around. I need to get changed for the day and want your passions high for tomorrow night."

Sindrick faced the wall and finished the drink. Eleanor slipped out the door again without saying goodbye, leaving him alone in the room. He sat the cup carefully on the floor. Whatever she put in the tea gave him a heightened focus.

He stood to get ready for the day and noticed the pile of clothes Eleanor changed out of in the corner. A metal chain glistened from the light spilling in through the slits in the window. It seemed to be beckoning him closer.

"She left it?" Sindrick said to himself as he pulled out the amulet.

He held the black stone up to the light. The strange allure of its dark aura forced him to stare at it for hours. Like a siren on the sea, he was seduced by the rock's impossible and hidden abilities.

Somewhere deep within it, a power greater than any he could fathom waited for him. It itched at his sanity. He wasn't sure if he was awake or dreaming as the rest of the morning and part of the afternoon wasted away.

The Salty Eleanor

The next day came too soon while Sindrick dozed off and on at the tavern. He spent most of the night celebrating with Dan and Jack again, so he decided to stay there overnight as his thoughts were wild with the upcoming event.

A banging on the door of the building made Sindrick stand up suddenly. The wedding party had arrived.

Eleanor entered first with her entourage close behind. Ribbons of white fabric wove between her hair and crisscrossed in front of her, highlighting her neckline in the intricate braids. Layers of sheer lace draped across the silk dress she wore. The beading stitched in the ivory corset went beyond the skill of any craftsman in the area.

She gave Sindrick a smile that caused his heart to ignite. All he wanted was to fall into her arms and curl up with her forever, surrounded in the nest of her hair.

"Your beauty is a vision beyond imagination," he said and staggered forward.

Then at once, he was on the ground. Strong arms lifted and dragged him to the back room.

"Give him this," Eleanor said as the others surrounded him.

A mug was shoved to his mouth, and the strawberry liquid slipped down his throat before he could respond. The men who grabbed him took off what he was wearing and dressed him in a clean robe. As his mind cleared, he recognized similar patterns to the fabric Eleanor wore, but his was not nearly as dazzling.

After more pushing and shoving to get ready, he joined his bride-to-be in the frozen air. It shook his senses sober enough to look among the crowd. He guessed everyone in Virfell was there for the spectacle. Malek entered to give his blessing right before the chief spoke.

Sindrick remained coherent enough to agree to the vows and kiss his new bride. Although their lips were not filled with as much passion as their first time in the tent, he felt her embrace in a new way. This time, she was his, completely. There would be no doubts if she wanted to be with him or not. And someday, they would journey to the frozen hills together when the best years of their lives were spent.

"You planned all of this in one day?" Sindrick asked as he escorted Eleanor to the reception banquet. "You are the most amazing and wonderful woman I have ever met. I am so honored to be your husband."

"I've wanted to be with you for a very long time. You won't be able to get away from me again." Eleanor quickly kissed his cheek. "There are a few more things we need to do before we head north, but I am impressed by this village's generosity. We won't need to sell anything from the cove for a while. We'll be able to spend the winter getting the shop ready."

"Oh no!" Sindrick's eyes went wide from the realization. "I forgot to get a cart for us."

"Had too much fun with your friends?" She raised an eyebrow. "Wait, you're serious, aren't you? Did you honestly forget about it?"

Sindrick could almost feel the animosity coming from her glare. He looked to the ground and nodded.

"So, instead of doing the one thing I asked while I was preparing everything else for our wedding, you spent the entire time at the tavern?"

"I wasn't there the whole time. I found your amulet," Sindrick confessed. "You left it behind, and I was studying it most of the day."

She placed a hand over the necklace and sighed. "I wondered why it wasn't in my bag when I came back. Were you able to find out more about the materials?"

"I tried, I honestly did. . . I'm sorry."

"I know." Eleanor slipped her arm around his and pulled him closer. "You'll have plenty of time to study it now. I shouldn't have put any responsibilities on you and left you alone with the amulet. I'd hoped it would be easier for you to understand."

They walked into the tavern full of expensive scents. The tables were lined with food and hungry faces. A few drinks later and the rest of the day fell into a blur of dancing and cheers. Whatever happened, Sindrick was glad he would be waking up next to the woman of his dreams from that moment on.

14

Winter in their new home was harsher than Sindrick expected. The road out of Virfell had already started to freeze over after their wedding. By the time they unloaded the gifts from the wedding, the path to northern town had become a mess of drifts and ice. Any attempt to gather more supplies would be risky.

Sindrick didn't mind the months of solitude with his new wife. The warmth from the forge was comforting, and he hardly noticed the time slipping by as the nights grew longer and colder. Evenings with Eleanor went beyond his wildest dreams.

Yet the mystery of the amulet nagged at the back of his mind as she only allowed him to examine it when she was present.

Eleanor liked to work at night and rest during the day. Sindrick's ability to hammer grew to a standstill, which allowed him time to formulate the design for a pair of bracers against the elements. They would create an invisible shell of protection around the user. The missing material was the right stone to blend with the metal. His memory of the cave grew hazy as the days wore on, but he was certain he saw the perfect ingredient there.

"You look tired," Eleanor said as she walked out of the bedroom and stretched. "Maybe you should lie down for a while."

Sindrick blinked from staring at the forge. His eyes had been watering, and he probably looked ready to pass out in his hunched position.

"You're always right." Sindrick reached for his tea, but it was already empty.

"Here, let me give you something new," Eleanor grabbed the cup and added a powdered mix into some fresh water. "I was working on this mixture last night. You're not the only one who's studied alchemy. I know you've had restless dreams. This will help your thoughts and muscles relax."

Sindrick nodded and took back his mug. With how tired he was, it wouldn't be necessary, but he drank the harsh mixture. It burned down his throat like strong alcohol.

The room spun from the quick reaction of chemicals to his brain.

The Salty Eleanor

He stumbled onto the bed and wrapped himself in for the night. But instead of falling asleep, his body seemed to lie dormant while his mind raced out of it. He struggled to regain control of his senses.

From the other side of the canvas walls, he heard Eleanor talking with someone. Sindrick forced himself up and managed to creep out of the bedroom.

The forge's glow was gone, and the area was completely dark except for an eerie light illuminating Eleanor. Her back was to him and covered in the strange black words that crawled along her skin.

"The way is open for me, but you cannot cross over," Eleanor said. Her voice echoed like she was in a vast cavern. "Something remains in your path. Can we complete the ritual on my side?"

"It will not be complete until your flesh meets ours," a voice responded, but Sindrick could not determine where it came from. "Be patient as we are patient. You are not the first."

"They were weak." Eleanor snarled. "I will become the vessel and the master of your power. We must find another way if he cannot unlock it." She held up her hand, grasping onto the amulet.

"The door will be revealed," the invisible voice said. "And Sindrick will open it for us."

He couldn't see the entity speaking with Eleanor but somehow felt its force staring right at him.

"Sindrick?" Eleanor asked as the words covered her body and encased her in darkness.

A blast of light hit Sindrick's eyes. He lifted his hand to cover them.

"Sindrick?" Eleanor said again. Her voice sounded normal and concerned. "What are you doing out of bed?"

She sat at his workbench, writing in one of her ledgers. The room had returned to its normal state, and she raised an eyebrow to Sindrick.

"I thought you were talking to someone else," he said and scratched his head.

"There's no one here but us."

"But you were standing there." Sindrick pointed to where he saw her in the vision. "It looked so real."

"I'm sorry." Eleanor approached him and put her hand on his arm. "The drink I gave you must not have worked. It was supposed to help you sleep, but you were likely dreaming while awake."

"You could be right. I do feel more awake." Sindrick rubbed his eyes to clear his mind. "What were you writing?"

"I've been working on a list of supplies. It's getting warmer, and the path to town should be open."

"Is it already spring?" He tried to keep his thoughts from the darkness before, but the nightmare wouldn't leave. "Do you mind if I ask you about the amulet?"

"I wouldn't mind at all," Eleanor said and gazed at him intently. "Do you need more of your sweet tea? I'm making extra for when I go to the village."

The thought of the strawberry and mint of Eleanor's tea made him nod unintentionally.

"I would understand the materials in the amulet better if you could describe more about where it came from in the elven woods," Sindrick said as she poured him a cup. "Were you there when the scavengers gave it to you? Did you see the place?"

Eleanor closed her eyes and seemed to be lost in an inner battle. "My parents lived west of the elven kingdom for a while. Most of the villagers warned us about an area that caused the war between the humans and elves—deep within the woods where the trees refuse to grow. It was an empty place." She took out the amulet, and the shadows around her shifted from the glow of the forge. "I should have taken more for myself. The remnants are lost now." She pressed the stone to her lips. "And yet, I feel the roots of something growing within this rock."

"I'll help you find it," Sindrick said and placed his hand over hers. "I know I'm close to discovering the true abilities of what you hold."

Eleanor smiled and held up the necklace. The lines under her eyes had darkened since their wedding. Sindrick initially thought it was due to the harsh winter, but something else was wearing them down, rotting away her spirit.

"I know you have been troubled as well," Sindrick said. "I am here to help you overcome it."

Eleanor's lips parted to speak, but nothing came out. The galactic wonder in her eyes faded. She blinked slowly and looked out the window.

"I should leave for town," she said abruptly and slipped the amulet back around her neck. "It will be light by the time I arrive there. I'm sure the path to the hidden cave is open too. You should look for gems while I'm gone."

"You know me too well," Sindrick said and gulped down the tea. "I need to craft more items if the roads are opening. We might get customers soon. Take your time. I'll need to use the anvil and forge."

Eleanor didn't respond and turned away coldly, leaving with a slam of the door. It shook the rocks on the table.

Sindrick took a deep breath to calm his nerves and stuffed small chunks of food into a large bag. He would need as much room as he could spare for the stones in the cave.

He grabbed a bottle of water to take with him and hopefully chase off the tea's dizzying effects. Downing it might have been a bad choice.

He took a couple swallows of water and stumbled into the morning light. The air froze his nostrils instantly. With a makeshift scarf, he covered most of his face and set off for the cliffs.

The spray from the sea brought a frigid gasp to the air. It hurried Sindrick's steps down the hidden path to the cave. Once inside, the echoing of the waves beating on the outer walls created an ominous tension, increasingly harder for him to ignore.

Sindrick focused on the prize of his search, the quartz. Yellow and golden shards sparkled before him. Their reflective glow continued to light up the area as if outside, even with the cloudy skies. It brought him a subtle tranquility.

He examined the rocks closer. If he combined the materials correctly, they would bring a calming aura to anyone who wore them. Fashioned into a wearable object, it could prove beneficial for any negotiation, and people would pay a hefty price for it. With Eleanor's skills in speaking, they could raise a small fortune with those items alone.

Sindrick cleared off the mud around the quartz to find its base. He carefully extracted a handful of shards with his pick. Simply holding them made him feel more at ease. Combined with the tea he consumed earlier, the room seemed to loosen beneath him, and his mind felt like it was floating to the ceiling. He quickly rested the materials within his bag.

As he remembered, one area of the cave held a collection of stones able to withstand any extreme temperature. A few pieces had already fallen away from the rest. They would be perfect for his bracers and for use in his alchemy studies.

A foul stench of mold and decay floated past him as he placed them in his bag.

Sindrick turned and peered into the vast cavern. It wasn't coming from the sea. Something else lurked in the depths of the hidden tunnels—an ethereal presence creeping into his imagination.

"Who's there?" Sindrick's voice echoed. "I am well armed and skilled in combat. It would be ill-advised to try attacking me."

The Salty Eleanor

The chill of someone watching him responded back. He had
lied about being well-armed. Although accustomed to his tools on
an anvil, his ability to use them in combat had been grossly
overstated.

"Where are you?" he asked quieter, unable to shake the
sensation of not being alone.

A ghostly voice broke the silence. It was almost inaudible due
to the rumbling of the ocean outside.

"Follow me to an endless night," the voice sung with the
rolling waves. "Leave behind your mortal fight. Delve into the
darkened depths, swim into the icy sea. Let your fears slip away
like the light."

The glow from the quartz stopped, and the space went dark.

Sindrick stumbled toward the entrance, tripping over
stalagmites jutting up from the ground. One tore through the
fabric on his pants and into his skin. He grabbed his leg to stop
the bleeding.

The voice was likely a lingering effect of the mixture Eleanor
gave him earlier, but he didn't plan on staying any longer to find
out. Disturbing the rocks might have woken something meant to
slumber in peace. Whatever entity spoke to him, it thrived in
darkness with no fondness for light.

Sindrick scrambled back to the forge and set to work on the gems he recovered from the cavern. He grabbed a few straps of leather to bandage his leg and used the remains to fashion an ornate belt with the calming stones. They brought a stillness to his mind, which was needed after his encounter in the cave.

He figured it would be best to wait for Eleanor's return before he ventured there again. He would have plenty to study with the amount of quartz he managed to scavenge. Given enough time, he could test their ability to protect the wearer against the elements. If he worked fast enough, the bracers could be ready before Eleanor came back from town.

However, that night, Eleanor did not return.

15

Sindrick paced around the anvil, wondering if he should look for Eleanor in town. She had not returned for three nights. He tried making some of her tea to keep his mind focused, but it wasn't the same.

Some of the local villagers had stopped by to peruse his works. They quickly talked down the price of what he hoped to sell. Sindrick used the effects of the calming belts he made on the patrons to his advantage and questioned them about Eleanor's whereabouts. However, none of them had seen her except in passing.

The dream of her holding the amulet kept invading his thoughts while he nervously braided his hair back. It had grown longer during the winter isolation, and Eleanor didn't seem to mind. She rarely commented on his appearance, only his actions.

"I should go," he said, convincing himself to leave the shop.

The door slammed into his hand as he reached for it. Crowell burst inside, breathing heavily.

"Sorry, friend," he said and grunted. "Wasn't expecting you to be right by the door."

"I'm all right." Sindrick shook his throbbing fingers. "Have you seen—" Eleanor slipped around Crowell before he could finish. "Eleanor? I was worried about you. Is everything okay?"

"I'm fine, but he is not," Eleanor said and pointed at Crowell. "I was in the village, and some of the locals were saying the pass had opened up. I decided to look for myself. That's when I found Crowell at death's door along the cliffs."

"How could anything get the jump on our captain?" Sindrick eyed Crowell suspiciously.

He hadn't noticed before, Crowell's arm was in a sling. A few bandages were wrapped around his legs.

The captain opened his mouth to speak but started coughing.

"Please, come in closer to the forge," Sindrick said and helped his friend ease onto a chair. "What happened to you?"

"It was the creature," Crowell said. "I found out about your wedding and decided to give you a piece of my mind. Then the beast from the shack came out of nowhere. I was right. It didn't die. It somehow learned from last time and got stronger." He clenched his fists and went into a fit of coughs.

"It's okay," Eleanor said and patted him on the back. "I can tell the rest."

Sindrick held back the pang of jealousy and stood beside her.

"The battle was more fierce this time, and he barely defeated it," she continued. "As soon as I found him, we went to a healer in town. I waited to make sure he would recover. Sorry, I was away longer than I planned. Did you get anyone to visit our shop? I told some people about this place."

"A few came and bought my latest work." He paused as Crowell was the last person he wanted to know about the hidden cave. "It took a bit of digging, but I found some new materials in this area."

Eleanor gave him a nod in acknowledgment of their secret.

"Our shop is already proving to be useful," she said and placed her hand on Crowell again. "You should let Sindrick know who you found on your travels. I'll get some drinks ready while you two catch up."

She rushed back outside before Sindrick could protest.

"You'll never believe what happened." Crowell slapped his leg and then groaned. "I came close to confronting Gostav, the troll king. I saw his ship in the distance."

"You're still alive, so I'm guessing you didn't cross cannons with him," Sindrick said.

"Something better happened." Crowell leaned forward to whisper. "I summoned up a creature to follow and destroy him. This time, it obeyed me. I was too far away to determine if it succeeded. My guess is that Gostav killed it, but I haven't heard any reports about the troll king being around since I worked my magic. I came back in hopes of getting a more effective spell."

"What about the other ships? I always thought the king traveled with an armada."

"Those rumors aren't true," Crowell said and sat back. "He was alone. I wish I could've fought him hand-to-hand."

"Maybe next time you will get the chance." Sindrick rested against his anvil and sighed. "I thought about informing you of our marriage, but I didn't want to send a ship in case you had found him. And, knowing you, you'd probably try talking me out of it."

"I'm surprised by how fast it happened. I didn't think she—" Crowell stopped as Eleanor entered with a bottle of rum and a large mug of tea.

"Here you are," she said, handing the tea to Sindrick and the rum to Crowell. "Did you tell Sindrick about your summoning abilities?"

"He's seen first hand what I can do," Crowell said and took a swig. "Thank you for not sending anyone out to inform me of the wedding. A courier ship would have given away my position. It wasn't easy to track him. Gostav's ship was fast, and their island is impossible to find."

"It wouldn't surprise me if it moved locations as well, like a floating vessel." Sindrick lifted the tea to his mouth.

The scent of Eleanor's mix calmed his anxiousness. Its warm contents relaxed the tightness in his throat from worrying over her the last few days.

"I'll find a way to kill them for good." A darkness came over Crowell's visage. "My powers grow stronger. Apart from the first ones, the creatures I summon have started to obey me. In the hidden depths of the sea lies what I need to wipe out the trolls. I just need to find it."

"Crowell's hoping we can aid him with some items," Eleanor said, interrupting his rant. "You had mentioned something to withstand the elements. Did you get anywhere with that idea while I was gone?"

"I'm currently working on the final design, but I did craft something for you." Sindrick hesitated before grabbing one of the belts. It might have been better to give the calming stones to Crowell, but there was no way the captain would wear such an ornate belt. "I created this to help when you are out. It should make everyone around you more pleasant and agreeable."

"It looks lovely." Eleanor tested it around her waist and set it gently on his workbench. "You two probably have more to talk about, and I'm exhausted. I need to rest for a while."

She withdrew to the bedroom. Although their home was too small to have a private conversation with Crowell, having an old friend nearby after the long winter was nice.

"So, the pass has opened up to Virfell?" Sindrick hopped up to sit on his workbench.

"There's some ice packed in places, but one could easily pull a cart through it. You should come back for a while. I know the others have been missing you."

"You can admit you've missed me too." Sindrick smiled.

Crowell shrugged. "I suppose I've been worried about my lackey. Also, you need to see Dan. He and Rena had their child, a son. They told me how to get up here and wanted to come themselves, but their boy is too young. It'd be best if you came down. I have a place you could stay if you like."

"I'll have to discuss it with my wife." Sindrick took another sip of the tea. It became hard to focus on anything but its taste. Whatever Eleanor used made it impossible to recreate. "Have Jack and Kate gotten together yet?"

"Not yet. It will likely be soon, but her family is worried about him providing for her." Crowell stood and stretched. "You did it right by marrying up. Eleanor is quite an amazing woman."

"She is. The rarest gem of them all." He shuddered at the thought of the words crawling across her skin and the voice in the cave. "There is something I might need your help with."

"You having problems in bed with her?" Crowell burst into laughter.

"Not that kind of problem." Sindrick felt his cheeks getting red. It had been some time since they were together. "Those spells you learned, can they protect you from unseen forces? There are odd things around here, and it would be good to defend myself better."

"Your fancy trinkets and alchemy aren't enough to keep the demons at bay, after all." Crowell grinned. "No need to fear, I'll learn you on some easy ones. Although, they say it comes at the price of your sanity."

"I've got plenty to spare," Sindrick said. "Unlike some others."

Crowell let out an overly-dramatic scoff. "There's nothing wrong with a little madness once in a while."

Eleanor stomped out of the room with a look that halted their conversation.

"I know you're excited to see each other, but can you keep it down?" she fumed. "I would like to get a little sleep."

"Sorry, dear," Sindrick said and looked to his feet.

"You two can get our cart ready," she said. "I'd like to take you up on your offer, Crowell. As soon as I wake up, we will leave for Virfell."

The men nodded in unison as she retired behind the sheets. They looked at each other and held back their snickering.

"You should probably recover a while longer before we leave," Sindrick whispered to Crowell and piled the spare blankets close to the forge. "There's not much to pack, and you probably can't do much with one arm."

Crowell tried to move his hand out of the sling but winced. "There's no point in arguing." He sighed. "Don't drink my rum. I'll need it on the way back."

Sindrick helped Crowell onto the makeshift bed and grabbed a bag. Most of what they needed was likely in the supplies Eleanor brought back from the village. After a few minutes of packing, he sat on the chair and found himself dozing off with the others.

16

The steep cliffs on either side of the passage made Sindrick feel like a floating leaf in a forest. They towered above his head with snow hanging over the edge, ready to come loose and cover the entire group as they traveled to Virfell. It encouraged them to move quickly on their journey.

The town's atmosphere had a less welcoming presence than when he left. Crowell seemed to be the only one happy about seeing him again. The people gave cruel glances to Eleanor, which made him want to slug each one of them. If not for the other two in his company, he likely would have helped them remember that scorning a blacksmith is a risky endeavor.

With clenched fists, he made it through the central part of town and to the massive harbor. Crowell's empty ship rocked gently from the wave break.

"You two can stay in my cabin," Crowell said as he motioned for the harbormaster. "I will stay below deck in the crew bunks if I'm not at the tavern."

"Captain, is there a problem?" the harbormaster asked, running up to him.

"Not at all." Crowell pointed at Eleanor and Sindrick. "These two will be staying on the ship with me for the time being. Please allow them access whenever they want."

"At your command." The harbormaster bowed and helped secure the gangway.

"Where's the rest of your crew?" Sindrick asked as he pulled the cart onto the deck. "Did you scare them off already?"

"After being on the hunt for so long, they're on a much-needed shore leave. Some stayed in Northeal. I like to stop there to resupply."

"We won't need to worry about interruptions then," Eleanor said and nudged Sindrick. "Thank you for allowing us to use your cabin. I know it is not a small gesture."

Crowell nodded and grabbed one of the boxes with his good arm. The other had been taken out of the sling, but he remained cautious with his movements. It gave him more pain than he was letting on. Appearances were everything when it came to commanding a ship.

They finished unloading the bags and crates of supplies into the cabin. Sindrick noticed Eleanor more inclined to grab the boxes Crowell was lifting than the ones he was struggling with. He tried to think of it as her way of showing gratitude for the lodging and not become too concerned about her attention towards the captain.

"Looks like you've been redecorating since the last time I was here," Sindrick said while the three settled around the dining quarters. "It's, dare I say, cozy?"

"If I remember right, we kept to the deck with it was storming outside," Crowell said. "You haven't been below in a while."

"And we're missing one of the crew being tied to the mast." Sindrick winked and broke off a hunk of bread.

"We can have that arranged. You missed your own midnight voyage." Crowell tried to laugh but ended up coughing.

"I'll pass," Sindrick said, grabbing a bottle of water to offer his friend. "Speaking of the one tied down, how are Dan and Rena?"

"I saw him at the tavern when I stopped in to ask about you two. It was hard getting any information from him, and he left shortly after he told me about your wedding. I'm guessing he doesn't get much time away from his child."

"Why don't you go and see if he's at the tavern?" Eleanor said with a yawn. "I'll need quite a bit of time to straighten up our new quarters and rest for a while."

"Good idea, I'll go with you and grab one of Jack's homebrews," Crowell said and stood up. He groaned. "On second thought, I should probably lie down as well. The trip back here took more out of me than I thought."

"I'm surprised you don't have the strength to boast about your encounter with Gostav," Sindrick said and stuffed some of the bread in his mouth. "Don't worry. I'll let them know."

"Once you get back, I may need your help with something." Eleanor gave him a sly grin. "But take your time. It's been too long since I've had uninterrupted sleep."

"I love you," Sindrick said and gave her a quick kiss on the cheek before heading to the tavern.

Although the idea of leaving her alone with Crowell gave him pause, he trusted Eleanor. She had vowed to be with him for their lifetimes.

"Well, I'll be a fae's wing," Jack exclaimed as Sindrick entered the tavern. "I thought you had been frozen up for the winter. Did Eleanor finally let you leave?"

"It was none other than our good captain. Crowell came up and let us know the pass was clear." Sindrick pulled up a stool next to his friend.

"That's an odd thing for him to do," Jack said, making room at the bar. "Of course, he's been acting weird ever since he started learning those spells."

"You know, it is strange that he would come all the way up just to check on us." Sindrick sat down slowly. "Maybe he was looking for the creature he summoned. It attacked him again, and Eleanor found him beaten up after the battle. He convinced us to come down and see Dan and Rena's son."

"Good luck with that." Jack poured him some of his latest brew. "She doesn't let anyone see the child much. Aldrnari is their treasure. I tried to convince Dan to be less protective, but that's like asking a fish to quit swimming."

"Crowell did say that the child takes up most of their time."

"They've got a newborn." Jack laughed. "No one's seen them for months. Speaking of children, have you and Eleanor sought a healer or anything to check on her?"

"Not yet. We haven't been together like that in a while." Sindrick took a drink and sneezed. "Man, what did you put in this?"

"It's more of a medicinal brew. Made it to cure what ails you. An ale for an ail is what I call it."

Sindrick took another swig. It tasted like rotten seaweed.

He breathed in deeply after sneezing again. The air smelled fresh and new. He hadn't felt so aware of his surroundings in quite some time.

"I've taken some of the healers' recipes and gave them my own twist," Jack continued. "Figured if I can't make good tasting alcohol, I can at least make something helpful. Some of our talks about alchemy inspired my mixing."

"It definitely helped clear my mind," Sindrick said with a half-smile. "I've been under a cloud for so long."

"I'm glad it perked up your gloom," Jack said and twirled a cup around in his fingers. "Anyway, I should probably get back to Kate. I'm supposed to help her family with a few things before tonight."

167

"Isn't this the time you normally show up at the tavern?" Sindrick looked outside. He couldn't remember Jack leaving so early.

"I need to go, okay? At least I tell you when I'm leaving." He looked at Sindrick like he wanted to say more, but he shook his head and walked out.

Jack had never been one for so few words. He treated Sindrick like he was a regular villager at the bar, not a lifelong friend. With the drink clearing his senses, he realized most of what happened after marrying Eleanor had become a blur in his memory.

Sindrick scanned the faces of the few patrons at the tavern. None of them looked familiar. For having the whole town attend his wedding, he started to feel like an outsider.

After a few more sips of Jack's brew, he stood to leave.

"Wait," someone said and caught his arm.

Sindrick turned to see a woman with a concerned look in her eyes. Her face was young but appeared to be hardened from many battles.

"I overheard you talking about someone named Eleanor," she said. "Are you her husband?"

"Yes, we were married before the winter," Sindrick said as the woman released her grip. "Why do you ask?"

"You don't know, do you?" She looked to the floor. "How could you know?"

"Do you know Eleanor? I don't remember seeing you in Virfell."

"I arrived here recently, but my captain told me all about her. She is the Eleanor every harbormaster and captain at least knows rumors about. Some say she admirals a hundred ships without being on board. Whatever she wants, she gets—or makes them pay for not giving it to her. Our captain insisted on coming here so she could help him with his summoning on the Stormeye."

"Stormeye?" Sindrick interrupted. "Your captain is Crowell of the Stormeye?"

"Yeah, he's the one." She bit her lip. "I probably shouldn't be saying this, but there's a deep sorrow within you. Please be careful. Crowell kept going on about his desperate friend being with the woman. I didn't know he'd be so handsome."

She smiled as Sindrick's thoughts swirled in confusion. He always assumed Eleanor hid something vital from him. It was during Dan's wedding when she first returned to Virfell, almost the same time as Crowell.

"Thank you," he said and forced a smile in return. "I need to find Crowell."

He didn't hear her response while he exited. All he could focus on was getting back to the Stormeye as quickly as possible.

The sun descended over the sea, giving its last glimmers of light. Sindrick could taste the salt spray as his senses lifted. For the first time since the wedding, his mind became clear, although not in a good way.

His chest tightened as he found the crew quarters to be empty. Something was going on, something terrible he should have suspected earlier. He wanted to be angry, but hurt filled him more.

A numbness entered him as he wandered toward the main cabin.

Crowell's voice was muffled through the door, "You said it wouldn't take you long."

Sindrick crept closer and pressed his ear against the wood.

"His ability is incredible, but we haven't unlocked it yet," Eleanor said. "It's only a delay. Let's not talk about him anymore. This is about us and our arrangement."

"You promised me the power to summon creatures from beyond our world." Crowell grunted. "I'm beginning to doubt their strength."

"Don't worry, you are getting more than we bargained for," Eleanor said coyly.

Their voices stopped as Sindrick crawled to the small window. There was no mistaking the two who were on the bed. Sindrick's wife and former friend gave in to their passions.

He staggered off the ship and headed back to town, wishing he noticed it sooner. Crowell destroyed everything he hoped to live for. He was always too late to discover the truth.

The town of Virfell seemed to mock him as he walked through its empty streets. He had no one to turn to or ask for help. Malek might take him back, but he felt too much shame to face his former master.

"No one will care if I leave," Sindrick muttered to himself and looked down at his bracers.

They would protect him through the cold night on the journey north. At least there he had something he could work on to keep his mind preoccupied. No one but Eleanor would wonder about him, and she was too busy with someone else to notice his departure.

He looked back one last time toward the place where his friend betrayed him. He wished Crowell taught him some sort of spell to curse them, but he had nothing. Only the rage and hurt he bottled up kept him company as he ventured north to his forge.

17

Hours turned to days while Sindrick remained alone. He tried to keep himself busy by forging new items, but the painful thoughts of Eleanor's betrayal stripped away his sleep. Many times he traveled down the path to the sea. When he reached the edge of the cliffs, he would look down the rock wall's expanse, wondering if he should end it all with another step.

His bracers were off by his side, hoping to feel the cold air, something other than the isolation from his closest friends.

He closed his eyes and pictured himself encompassed by the sea, restless as his wife's heart. She was never his.

He convinced himself of it being his fault she left, foolishly trying to tame her wayward heart. In his cowardice, he ran from her and the dark presence he could have saved her from. He couldn't forgive himself for not being able to understand the black stone she wore.

"Why didn't you fight for her?" he questioned the silence.

He wished for rain as his cheeks were dry from too many tears. There was no need for more.

"You are not a man, Sindrick!" he cried out to the waves. "You have lost the only one worth finding."

He could almost hear Eleanor calling back to him. Her voice sounded like it floated back with the rushing tide.

No, it was her voice, coming from behind him.

"Sindrick? What are you doing out here?" Eleanor ran up to him. "I searched all over Virfell. Someone finally told me you'd left on the trail back north. Why did you abandon me?"

"Eleanor, you know why I had to leave." Sindrick held in his sadness. "I saw you and Crowell together on the ship. You don't have to hide it."

"It's not what you think," she said, reaching out to him. "I became sick after you left and fell. He was helping me to the bed."

"Why do you continue to lie to me?" he asked and stood straighter. "You've never been honest with me since we met. I'm not convinced anymore that you were ever close to my family."

"You still don't remember me from when we were little." She crossed her arms. "How can you know me now?"

Sindrick clenched his fists and wanted to punch himself for his memory. She was right.

"I want to, but you never let me close to you," he said quietly.

Before he said another word, her hand slapped across his cheek.

"I let you be with me multiple times," Eleanor said as Sindrick backed away, dangerously close to the edge of the cliff. "You don't know what I gave up. All I asked was for you to understand this." She pulled out the amulet and held it in his face. "You ruined everything with your incompetence. You were supposed to have some sort of renowned skill in alchemy and understand gems, yet you couldn't give me a clue to this one's properties. Did you even try, or were you too busy in your own work to do what I asked?"

"I. . . I'm sorry," Sindrick could barely get the words out.

"You wouldn't be sorry if you had any capability in what your father did."

"I can't do this anymore." His heart hurt more than her strike. "It was a mistake for us to be together. Just leave. It's what you were planning to do anyway."

175

Sindrick instantly regretted what he said. He could see the pain in her eyes. They welled with tears.

Eleanor stroked the smooth stone of the amulet while she stepped back.

It glowed with the same dark intensity he witnessed in the vision. However, this time there was no mistaking the change in her composure. He was fully awake.

Lines formed across her skin into inky words, crawling up her neck and across her face. Her eyes turned pitch black and filled with the same dark aura as the amulet.

"You will find a way to release them," her voice echoed around him. "I made a promise to open the way, and I will have their power. We will not be driven back again!"

Eleanor screamed and rushed at Sindrick.

He stumbled out of the way and felt his hands on her back. In the chaos, he couldn't tell if he was pushing or trying to grab her. He twisted around at the edge of the cliff to see her descending to the sea below.

Her limbs reached out with nothing to hold onto but air as her cries amplified to a ghastly volume. The trail of smoke from the amulet surrounded and engulfed her completely when she reached the bottom, hitting where the sea met the land.

Whatever remained of her body washed away into the icy depths of the waters.

The chill from the shock left Sindrick as a new shudder took over. He had caused all of this. He had murdered his wife.

"No!" He screamed. "You can't be gone. What have you done? What have I done? Please come back. I'm sorry."

Sindrick fell to his knees, shaking with fear. The waves churned from the rising tide, and his ears rang with the memory of her cries. Because of the black mist from the amulet, he didn't see her hit the bottom and hoped she was somehow unharmed.

He continued to stare into the watery abyss until his eyes hurt from the saltwater spraying into them. The hairs on the back of his neck stood up as a new presence lingered nearby.

He spun around and peered across the open field. Although he couldn't see anyone, Eleanor may not have traveled alone.

Sindrick crawled back from the edge. He had to hide.

The wind beat against him as he scurried down to the cave. His fallen wife knew about the hidden place, but her voice was silenced. He could stay there for as long as he needed and fashion new materials with the endless supply of gems.

The mouth of the cavern swallowed his sanity as Sindrick entered. The harsh stone became colder and less enticing than when he first discovered it. Nothing could make him shake the thought that he was a murderer. At the least, he was a coward for not saving her. The details of the accident remained a blur.

As he ventured farther in, a new realization made his sickness worse. He couldn't shape the stones into usable objects. Everything held fast in its place and would not break loose with his bare hands. His tools remained at the forge. Without them, the cave became more like a prison—one he could not escape. He could only delve deeper, hopefully finding something strong enough to loosen the gems.

"What have I done?" he repeated to himself.

The room gave no reply as its darkness continued to embrace him, not wanting him to leave but to get lost in the cavern.

As he wandered the tunnels, Sindrick noticed the path getting brighter.

The quartz glowed with a reddish hue, hardly noticeable from the outside. It provided him enough light to make out the strange shapes on the walls. They reached out to him, but the illusions never touched him.

Dirt, instead of rock, muffled his footsteps. The waves from the outer seas ceased in this underground ecosystem. Sindrick thought he felt the brush of plants in the eerie red glow.

He stopped, finding an area of smooth rock to rest.

Nothing seemed to matter anymore. His forge would be considered cursed, and no one would want anything to do with him.

"I should rot in here," he said and covered his face. "I don't deserve a proper burial. She will never have one." The image of Eleanor covered in the black words flashed through his mind. "What was in that amulet?"

Sindrick rubbed his hands across the surface he sat on. A sharp prick in his finger from a splinter caused him to draw it back. The material seemed to pulse with his heartbeat as a strange sensation entered him.

He spun off the seat and inspected it closer. It was not rock but a type of wood. In the dim light, it appeared to be an ancient root system, molded together with the rocks and metals in the earth.

Within the recesses of his mind, the elements revealed more of their properties to him. Not only lightweight, the wood could withstand massive amounts of energy and any storm that tried to weaken its structure.

As much as Sindrick pulled at it, the material would not pry loose from the system holding it in place. Most wood split and cracked off. This one remained like a forged plate of metal. He pictured a new vessel crafted from his alchemy and blacksmith abilities—his greatest work.

"Forged wood," he muttered to himself. "I'm sure I could do it."

He squinted from the redness in the room while he looked across it. The entire area had been gifted with the material. There was more than enough to craft a ship so he could escape the cave unnoticed.

Although he had never created anything of its magnitude, every fiber inside him longed to produce the unshakable craft. And the hidden lake within the cave would house it until he was ready to leave. Crowell had taught him the basics of sailing, and he had steered the Stormeye before.

"This was all because of Crowell." Sindrick clenched his teeth. "He led Eleanor astray. If he hadn't been around, she wouldn't have fallen for him in the first place."

The Salty Eleanor

The last place she was seen in Virfell was likely on Crowell's ship. Unless she told Crowell, no one would know she went up to the cliffs. She liked to go wherever she pleased without informing anyone, so there was a chance she ventured alone.

Sindrick needed to get his tools to fashion the ship. Working on it would give him enough time for people to give up the search for him and Eleanor. Yet getting what he needed from the forge would be nearly impossible if someone was waiting for her return.

"I have nothing else to lose," he whispered and wandered toward the exit of the cave.

18

The twilight hours of the late evening hindered Sindrick from seeing clearly. It was unlikely anyone else would be able to find the path back to his forge without the aid of a light. Luckily, he knew his way in the dark once he reached the top of the cliffs, where Eleanor fell.

Sindrick waited a few more hours until the night grew late. He slipped through the shadows and down the road, keeping a close watch for any lights along his way. It would be difficult to explain himself if he was caught wandering alone.

As he crept up to the building, he noticed a soft glow inside. Someone had the forge going without the use of his rocks. They were using a primitive fire with wood.

The crisp scent of the burning pine pierced the air while he hid in the pile of rubble outside the house, checking for any movement. If Crowell had come up with Eleanor, he would not be waiting inside for her. They would have planned to meet somewhere less suspicious.

Sindrick snuck closer to the window, avoiding the light.

"What are you doing?" a strange voice came from behind him.

Sindrick froze. It didn't sound like Crowell, but he had many in his crew. It made sense to bring a small escort up with Eleanor and bring Sindrick back to Virfell, by any means necessary.

"Are you the one who lives here?" The man stepped closer, illuminated by the glow from the window. He held a stack of freshly chopped wood.

"I was. . . passing by and noticed the light on." Sindrick looked back toward the cliffs. "I've been on the road for a while. Do you own this place?"

"Not exactly," the man said and sat the wood down. He tried to unbuckle the strap on his ax without being seen. "I'm watching this place until the owner returns. I was told to report anything suspicious. Why are you out on these paths?"

"I'm sorry," Sindrick said and stepped into the light, holding his hands up to show he was unarmed. "I should have been honest before. I am an apprentice to the man who lives here," he lied. "He's been missing for a while, and I wanted to make sure the building was safe. When I saw the fire going, I thought he returned without telling me."

"I see." The man rubbed his beard and leaned forward. "You do look a bit soft around the eyes. Come in and warm yourself. I've got a pot brewing."

"Oh, I wouldn't want to be a bother," Sindrick said and looked to his feet. "Although I wouldn't mind checking up on the place. My master was quite particular about his tools."

The man opened the door and motioned for Sindrick to enter, quietly snapping the strap over his ax.

However, the weapon kept Sindrick's focus. He would need to move quickly to recover his tools and escape back to the cliffs.

Once inside, he noticed the place looked like someone had busted in and rummaged through his belongings. The rocks that he neatly organized on his workbench were scattered across the floor. Pieces of his chair had been broken off and used as fuel for the fire. Crowell had to be behind it.

"I shouldn't stay long," Sindrick said. "It's already late in the night, and I need to return to the village."

"Of course, of course." The man stared at him intently and walked over to the kettle boiling over the fire. "I do apologize for the mess. Your master must have left in a hurry. It was like this when I arrived. Tompkins wanted me to check on the place."

"Thank you for doing so," Sindrick said and glanced out the window. Crowell was likely lurking nearby, waiting for an opportunity to grab him. "How's the soup coming?"

"It's nearly done," the man said and turned back to the fire.

Sindrick used the distraction to smuggle his hammer and a small chisel. It wouldn't be much, but it was enough to create other tools he needed from inside the cave.

"These are some unique stones," he said, picking up his crystals. "I bet they'd be worth a substantial amount to the right buyer." He placed most of them back but palmed a few of the fire stones, slipping them into his pouch. "How long have you lived up here?"

"Oh, I've been here and there," the man said and shrugged. "I do a lot of traveling, so I haven't been in these parts much. I was good friends with Tompkins in the past. His family was suspicious of the people who lived here."

"I see." Sindrick turned to the window and acted like he was looking out while he snuck a few more tools into his bag. "I must apologize again. I've lost track of time. I should get going."

"The problem is that Tompkins went missing." The man forcefully grabbed Sindrick's shoulder.

Instinctively, Sindrick spun around with his elbow and struck the man in the temple. The man shook it off and gritted his teeth. Before he could counter-attack, Sindrick threw one of the stones.

It drew blood from a square hit to the jaw. The man reeled back but jabbed at Sindrick. The punch rolled off his shoulder while he turned from it. A second jab exploded in his gut.

Sindrick grunted and managed to block another hit. He swung wildly. The knuckles of his fingers struck the man's throat.

The man collapsed to the ground, gasping for breath. A quick kick to the side caused him to stumble over, defeated.

Without looking back, Sindrick bolted out the door and down the road to town. When he was far enough, he doubled back into the trees, sneaking toward the hidden cave.

He stopped at the edge of the sea and looked across the waves.

Crowell would never be able to find the cavern on his own. Sindrick hoped Eleanor kept the place secret as she promised, being faithful to at least one of her vows. The image of them together in bed burned a scar in his memory.

The strange quartz seemed to welcome him as Sindrick entered the mouth of the cave. They were glowing from before, like sentinels watching over a fortress. Their intrigue eased his despair as he sought to discover their properties.

A small ridge led across the open cavern, passing by the tunnel leading to the red room with the hardened wood. The narrow walkway continued to wrap around the back, where the waters came close to it but never spilled over. The perfect location to construct his ship.

"What do you possess?" he said, getting closer to the glowing stones.

The rocks were not a singular material but a tiny collection that worked together. If combined properly, they would be brighter than regular fire. The light would be a relief for his eyes from the numbing red where he needed to extract the wood.

Chiseling the stones out of their locations, he fashioned them together with strips of fabric. His small orb illuminated the tunnel. Although parts of the passage dipped down, it remained straight, which would work in his favor to bring out the wooden planks.

Finding any weaknesses in the rock around them proved to be a complicated task. The roots would not budge from their location. Sindrick found the whole room to be one massive block of wood.

His hands were weary, and a soft glow from the dawn outside spilled into the tunnel by the time he loosened one. It stretched the full length of the room but was lighter than he imagined. He took out more boards to get an idea of their size.

He had never sailed in anything smaller than the ship Crowell designed. Yet somehow, the captain managed to run the Stormeye entirely on his own. The crew was likely there to clean or help with security when it docked—recruited more for their company than for sailing.

"I'll need a place below deck to store my materials," he said and sat down to draw out his ideas.

Working on the ship kept his mind preoccupied. The elements in the wood spoke their intended design to his subconscious. With speed and precision, the vessel took shape. He almost forgot about the tragedy. But as the days wore on, Eleanor seemed to whisper at him from the shadows.

Sindrick finished forging together the shell of the hull and leaned against a wall near the entrance to the cavern. For too long, he had worked without proper rest. His muscles and mind ached from being overworked.

He closed his eyes when a clear voice pierced his ears.

"I will return for you," the voice said, floating sweetly into the cave.

It echoed within the barren expanse and forced him to sit up. The tone was unmistakable. Eleanor spoke through the waves.

"Madness," her voice floated down to him from nowhere. "Madness of a murderer."

"I am no murderer," Sindrick muttered and looked across the dim glow of the cave.

The red haze gave some aid to the darkness, but he left the light orb where he extracted the wood in the other room. He wanted to rush back to grab it, yet fear held him in place.

"You will never rest," the voice returned. "You will drift forever with me. The one you killed."

Sindrick shook his head. It had to be exhaustion.

"You cannot get rid of me," the voice said louder and more aggressive.

Sindrick grabbed his hammer and stood up. In the corner of his eye, he caught a movement in the shadows. Something was hunched over, staring at him.

A woman, shrouded in darkness and holding her legs to her chest, rocked back and forth. Her form faded between the shadow and physical realms. Sindrick couldn't make out her face, but the words tattooed across her skin caused his heart to race.

The woman leaned forward, and Eleanor's eyes stared back at him.

Sindrick shrieked and fell against the wall. His vision blurred from the blow to his head, and just as quick, the woman disappeared.

He walked somberly to where her ethereal form sat.

"There's no one here," he whispered to himself. "I am alone."

The one he wished to be with would be forever gone. His only company in the cave was the ghost of her memory. He gripped his hammer tighter and vowed to finish the ship.

The Salty Eleanor

The forged vessel surpassed Sindrick's hopes in its size. The more he had worked, the larger it became. He envisioned the massive boat floating effortlessly along the seas. Its impenetrable material of wood and metal could hold it together for centuries.

It took a few tries, but he managed to position it onto a set of logs that he used to move the ship. The sharp boards cut through the stone floor, creating a slide into the water instead of the rocks damaging the surface of the hull.

Sindrick braced himself against the rail. Yet the ship hardly tipped from the displacement of the surface. It seemed like it was holding its breath inside the tranquil cove, ready to be set loose and explore the endless seas.

Giving one last force of strength, Sindrick hoisted the mast.

However, there was no fabric to create sails. He sat back in defeat. Everything else he could craft, but without them, it wouldn't get far from land.

"It was all in vain," he said and held his head in his palms. "I couldn't understand your amulet. Now this ship I made for you will never be complete."

The cave seemed to mock him. He needed to get away.

"You will never escape me," Eleanor's voice whispered into his mind. "I'm coming to show you our new home."

The sound echoed through the cavern, "Our home—madness."

Sindrick breathed out slowly, uncertain if it was Eleanor's voice or his own taunting him.

"I shouldn't be alone," he said and finished the inscription on the ship, giving it a name to his regret—his past life.

A harsh breeze blew into the cave. It had become colder outside. Pouring over his work on the ship made him lose track of the seasons. The pass would likely freeze over soon, and he would be stuck for good.

"I'll be free from you," Sindrick said to the empty cavern and put on his bracers.

He knew the perfect tailor to help him craft the large fabric. Convincing Dan to remain quiet about its purpose would be tricky, but not as difficult as trying to get through Virfell without being noticed. Crowell likely told everyone what happened at the cliffs.

Stepping into the sunlight nearly blinded him. He wrapped a cloth over his forehead and pulled a hood over his furs. It would help him hide his shame as well.

The Salty Eleanor

Focusing on the ship had been a good distraction, but the reality of Eleanor's death would be unavoidable. Everyone would ask, and he needed to have a reason for being gone so long.

"I was looking for Eleanor," he rehearsed to himself as he started down the road. "She's been missing since she was last on Crowell's ship."

19

Taking the outside paths around Virfell, Sindrick crept up to Dan's house and peeked inside. The darkened room gave no clue as to where the residents might be. Sindrick repositioned the warm scarf across his face and glanced around to make sure no one was watching.

"Hello?" he whispered while knocking softly on the door.

A slight creak responded while the door moved back. It was unlocked.

Sindrick stood frozen at the threshold. They had often entered each other's homes unannounced, but with a small child inside, he didn't want to risk making too much noise.

He pressed slowly on the door to let it swing open enough to glance inside. It remained dark and silent.

"Dan? Rena? Are you home?" he called out a little louder.

A rush of emotions hit him from the memory of his last visit to the home. The taste of strawberry and mint tea returned to his tongue. There was something more in Eleanor's drink he couldn't place, a hidden component that caused him to want it again. He hadn't been the same since she offered it to him.

He licked his lips and stepped inside.

The abrupt sound of scraping across the floor made him jump back. A piece of parchment blew past his foot. He peered down to see a sketch of Jack and Kate, announcing their wedding. Everyone would be there tonight, including the owners of the home.

Sindrick departed quickly and ducked into one of the alleys. He grabbed a few discarded blankets to disguise his regular coat.

The noise from the tavern grew louder as the night wore on. Sindrick waited until everyone would be too drunk to recognize their own hand before entering.

"Dan, I need to talk to you," he said, finding his friend in a staring contest with his drink.

"Sindrick?" Dan leaned in close. "Are you actually here or some kind of ghost? I've had too many spirits already."

"It's me, and I need your help."

"Don't we all?" He smiled and handed Sindrick his mug. "You have to drink all of this before we talk more—all of it. I can't have another sip, and I can't waste it. It would be a shame."

"One drink, but then I need you to come with me." Sindrick took a swig of the bitter liquid. The barkeeper had watered it down for the late-night crowd. "Come with me while I finish this. I'll help you walk."

"Where are we going?" Dan hiccuped and hopped off his chair. "And where have you been? Crowell said to let him know if you returned. His mood changed, really changed. Jack said we should keep an eye out before he finds you. Ever since you went missing, everyone's acted crazy. Jack's been weird with Kate, and I thought they were going to end it. Instead, they got married. It happened fast. Is Eleanor with you? Crowell wanted us to watch for her too."

Sindrick breathed out a sigh of relief. Crowell must not have been with Eleanor on that fateful day.

"It has been a long time since I saw. . . my wife." The words were harder to say than Sindrick expected. "She was helping Crowell on his ship. I haven't seen her since then."

"That's why I was skeptical about him looking for her," Dan said and leaned closer. "Some of the townsfolk said she was on his ship for a while before she started asking us about you. Jack was pretty sure she came to Virfell with him the night before my wedding. I didn't want to say anything about it because you seemed happy with her."

"I wish you would have told me sooner," Sindrick muttered as they walked out of the tavern. "She's not coming back, and I hope Crowell doesn't either."

"He's around here somewhere. He showed up, trying to convince Jack to go on a midnight voyage, but we both told him no. Remember what he did to my finger?" Dan grabbed Sindrick's arm. "Do you think he would summon more things to attack us?"

"Given what I'm discovering about him, it wouldn't surprise me."

Sindrick stopped and looked across the deserted streets. Crowell and Eleanor had been plotting against him the whole time. He needed to get away, far away from the pain of his past.

"I need your help building something big, like a giant tent," he said, leading Dan to the tailor's shop.

"Canvas tents are quick and easy. I am great at making fabric things." Dan perked up and smiled. "Were you at the wedding? It

197

was amazing to watch the fire twirlers again. Although the ceremony wasn't as good as mine—or yours. Rena is out walking with our son, Aldrnari. She's pregnant again already. We're going to have a bushel full."

"Honestly, I'm happy for you two." Sindrick checked to make sure no one was around the building. "You are a turning out to be a great father, and your shop is looking better by the day."

"Thank you, but we need to get back to the tavern soon. Rena will start looking for me if I'm not at the party. She stayed to watch the fire dancers with Aldrnari and then had to get away from the noise. She wasn't going to be gone from the celebration long."

"This should be quick." Sindrick didn't want to be in Virfell any longer than he needed to if Crowell was in town.

Dan fumbled for the key and finally unlocked the entrance. The tailor's shop was a lot smaller than Sindrick remembered, and it was almost empty.

"Where is everything?" he blurted out. "I thought there were sails and large canvases in here."

"We haven't worked on one of them in a while." Dan scratched his head and sat on one of the stools. "Most of what we do is mending. There should be enough scraps for a smaller tent, not the big one you wanted."

"A small one won't work," Sindrick said. "I need it to be the size of a sail."

"I'm not sure if we have the right material to make something that massive." Dan leaned back against the wall. "You know, you shouldn't give up on finding Eleanor. We were worried about you two at first, but I noticed how you were around her. You were always too serious about everything, and she made you smile a little more. Don't worry. She'll turn up somewhere."

Sindrick nodded as he turned his gaze to the dark streets. The thought of her appearing in the cave made his knees tremble, and he had to sit.

"Promise me you won't disappear again," Dan said and pointed at Sindrick. "That's what I hated most about her. I know Crowell says he's your best friend and all, but I miss being around you. We grew up together, and you've always helped me. Jack said it's not the same with you gone." He leaned in closer with his breath reeking of alcohol. "We tried to get rid of her once."

"What do you mean?" Sindrick's chest tightened. "Did you do something to her?"

"Oh no." Dan laughed. "We told her you fancied one of the girls in the tavern. This was well before you two ever got the cabin up north. It probably didn't help when you went away for a while to find the place. I think she found out we were messing with her."

"I'm sure she knew it was a lie. She was the queen of them," Sindrick whispered to himself.

The faint sound of her laughing crept in from the shadows around him. He shook his head to clear it off and frowned at his misfortune. There was no escape from her.

"So you don't have anything large enough for a sail?" he asked.

"Nope, sorry friend." Dan stood up and put his hands on his hips. "You should take Crowell's. Wouldn't that be something? The great captain burgled by a blacksmith."

"Is his ship at the port?"

"It should be. I saw him wandering around before the ceremony with a wild look in his eyes. He's the last one to be single and probably wanted to take advantage of it." Dan nudged Sindrick with his elbow. "Hey, you could also see if anyone on his ship knows where Eleanor went."

"You're full of great ideas." Sindrick rubbed his hands together. "You should get back to the tavern. I'll see what I can find out. Please don't tell anyone I'm back in town. I don't want people to be worried about me on Jack and Kate's big day."

"Stay safe," Dan said and chuckled. "Could you imagine what Crowell would do if you stole his sails? I might have to do it myself someday."

"I'm sure he deserves it," Sindrick said while they slipped out of the building.

He made certain Dan started in the right direction toward the tavern and escaped into the shadows. The night air gripped his lungs, forcing him to breathe heavily during the search for Crowell's ship. The sails would be perfect for getting his vessel on the sea and for keeping Crowell grounded.

An eerie quiet on the docks made Sindrick glance behind him multiple times to see if he had been followed. Since most of the town was at the celebration, the harbor's security was scarce. Sindrick snuck closer to Crowell's ship and waited behind a box of crates. If anyone stirred on deck, he would see them.

After he convinced himself it was empty, he summoned up the rest of his courage and crept across the gangway's squeaking boards.

The sails swung listlessly in the night sky, ready to be used for another journey. As Sindrick approached them, he noticed the door to the cabin remained open.

He stopped, ready for the captain to spring out and grab him. The boat rocked and caused the door to swing wider, revealing the unoccupied chamber. Nothing but memories of the betrayal between Crowell and Eleanor remained inside.

The blankets on the bed were tossed, and a large number of empty bottles clanged from the rocking waves. Beside them was an open book. Sindrick couldn't tell if it was a collection of maps or reports of the captain's exploits on the seas. Whatever it was, he hoped it would reveal more of Eleanor's past and the plan she devised.

As he reached for it, something moved in his peripheral vision.

"You're back early," a woman's voice called to him from the entrance. "I told you not to worry about the—"

She stepped out from the threshold and into full view. Sindrick recognized her from the tavern, one of the Stormeye's crew.

"Hey, you're not supposed to be here," she said and brandished her sword. "Crowell didn't mention anything about new recruits this landing."

"I've sailed with him before and just talked to him at the wedding," Sindrick said and held his hands up. "He asked me to find his maps, so I could show him where I found some treasure further north."

"You do look a little familiar." She tilted her head to the side. After a long stare, she clicked her sword back into its sheath. "Everything's fine and ready to sail when he gets back."

"Good to hear," Sindrick said and looked for a way out. "I should inform him. He's waiting back at the tavern."

He walked past her and started for the gangway.

"The tavern!" The woman grabbed his arm and spun him back around. "You're the husband."

"No, you must have me mistaken—"

Before he could say more, her fist struck him hard in the forehead.

The next sensation was the smell of moldy boards on the deck as he collapsed. She shouted something else at him, but it floated past with the rest of the world while he slipped from consciousness.

20

The rocking of the waves subsided as Sindrick felt like he was standing. He tried to steady himself, but the ropes around his hands held them fast behind his back.

"Where am I?" he wondered aloud while he blinked.

Complete darkness surrounded him. There was no light for his eyes to adjust. He wasn't entirely sure he had them open.

"The veil is thinning," a melodic voice said through the silence. "We must be closer than I thought, or you are near one drawing power from our realm."

The shadows around him parted like curtains to reveal who spoke to him, Eleanor.

Sindrick gasped. "How? How are you here?"

He tried to back away, but her form came closer to him.

"I wondered the same for you." Her blackened eyes stared into his until he fell to his knees. "But you are not here."

Eleanor frowned and held her hand close to Sindrick's chest.

"I cannot bring your complete form here," she continued. "But it merely delays the inevitable. I can sense the walls between our realms weakening. Some places I can gaze into already."

"You came back to me for a brief moment," Sindrick said, breathing slowly to focus. "I saw you in the cave."

"You did?" Eleanor grinned. "She was an echo of what I left behind, a reflection off the glass. Something else must be pulling our worlds closer than I thought."

Sindrick coughed as his face suddenly dripped with saltwater.

"You were watching me?" He strained against the ropes, trying to wipe away the sting in his eyes.

"I sense our powers being called upon. The time is not right." Eleanor stepped closer. "I will be the one to drag you here. No one else can have you."

Sindrick longed for her words to be spoken out of love, but an eerie chill ran down his spine.

She crouched behind him and whispered into his ear. "Wake up and be free."

His binds loosened around his wrists. The world shook around him while his mind returned to the deck of Crowell's ship.

"He's coming to," the woman who hit Sindrick said. "We don't have time. Do it now."

Sindrick was thankful she didn't slug him again and squinted to see her standing next to Crowell. He muttered in a strange language to the waters. It sounded similar to the inflections he used when he summoned the birds out of the sea.

A sharp tilt of the boat caused a wave to splash onto Sindrick's face. He coughed and instinctively tried to wipe his eyes. His hands slipped free from the ropes.

He quickly put them behind him and glanced up to see if anyone noticed he was unbound.

The summoning spell kept their attention. Crowell lifted his hands while the woman gasped.

"Is that supposed to happen?" she asked and took a few steps away from the edge.

Sindrick's gaze followed hers with increasing worry.

Off in the distance, a giant and disfigured sea monster floated in midair. It grew closer to the ship at an alarming rate. An invisible wall stopped it suddenly.

Crowell turned to the woman with a concerned look.

"I knew we should've gone out into open water," he said. "It can't approach—"

The shark-like creature swimming in the air began to vibrate into a blurry form. It stretched to create a humanoid shape and floated through the barrier.

"No! You're supposed to attack him!" Crowell shouted and pointed at Sindrick.

The beast latched onto Crowell and merged into his flesh. The body shook violently as it bulged and grew in size. Crowell's teeth became jagged while he cried out in pain.

Sindrick rolled toward the gangplank and sprinted away, not looking back to see the final transformation. He could hear the shouts fading as his heart pounded in his chest. Whatever Crowell summoned became part of him, and there would be no way to fight it without a stronger weapon, the type of weapon Sindrick was skilled in crafting.

Sindrick didn't stop running until he reached the threshold of Malek's forge.

He hoped his former master was already home for the night. It was impossible to determine the time. Clouds covered the sky, and he didn't know how long he had been unconscious.

"Are you in?" Sindrick called out and knocked on the door.

He listened for a while, but there wasn't any movement on the other side. He stared off toward the harbor. The howling of the local dogs let him know something had entered the town.

As he reached around to get the hidden key to the shop, the door swung open.

"Who's there?" Malek said, stepping out with a large sickle in his hands.

Sindrick jumped back and put his hands out. "Easy, Malek. It's me."

"Sindrick? Is it you, boy?"

"Yes." He checked behind him again. "Can I come in?"

Malek stepped aside and motioned for him to enter. "Sorry about the sickle. There are strange rumors around town."

Sindrick thanked him with a nod and slipped inside. The familiar scent of smoke and metal shavings eased his mind. He knew every tool in the building and every hiding place.

"What brings you here so late?" Malek asked, hanging the sickle by the door.

The Salty Eleanor

"I'm not sure if you heard, but Eleanor is missing, and Crowell is after me," Sindrick said. "I need a place to stay for a while. However, I could ask you the same. You don't normally stay so late at the forge."

"I have the same amount of work, but I am getting slower. Your help was invaluable."

Sindrick looked out the window and sighed. "I have something to ask of you, and I promise I'll find a way to pay you back."

Malek placed his hands on Sindrick's shoulders. "You don't need to repay me for anything. The years you stayed on as an apprentice enlightened me. You have a rarer gift than any item you could forge, one you haven't understood yourself. The worth of your mind outweighs any gem or metal you could give me."

A tear formed in Sindrick's eye. It was exactly what he longed to hear, but too late. His master could never know who he truly was—a murderer.

"Thank you, Malek," he managed to say. "I need you to leave for a while. Please, don't ask why. I need to create something alone."

"I understand," Malek said and gathered his coat. "You do what you must. Your solitude is your strength, but don't let it become your prison."

Malek wandered out of the building, and Sindrick turned to the glowing forge. There would be no more time to delay. He had to kill Crowell or be killed by the beast within the captain.

Sindrick hoped Malek hadn't gotten rid of his earlier works. He had nearly forgotten about the ruby sword. Most of the form was finished, but it needed to be sharpened.

From the far wall, he caught the glint of red gems. The sword had been recast and bent to resemble an ornate scabbard. A customer must have seen the blade and liked the metal for a different order. It was the opposite of what Sindrick needed.

He grabbed it and used an iron rod to lower it back into the forge. It didn't get hot enough to properly shape when he pulled it out, but there was no time. Shrieks of frightened villagers outside let him know Crowell was getting closer.

The clanging of his hammer on the cold metal made him wince, ready for it to crack.

"There you are!" a voice boomed.

It caused Sindrick to slam down on the blade, shattering it and his chance to defend himself.

"I know what you did." Crowell glared through the window. "Her words came to me from the other side."

Crowell's eyes produced a black aura, and his muscles bulged under the thin skin. Something possessed him. He no longer sounded like himself. Any rational side of him was swallowed up in the dark magic.

Sindrick took one of the iron rods and rushed to the door, wedging it shut.

It didn't slow Crowell's attack. Fragments of the wooden slab burst open. Sindrick scrambled back to the forge, grabbing whatever he could find to defend himself.

Crowell moved with unholy speed and batted down whatever was held up to him.

Sindrick managed to dodge Crowell's advancing dagger. He reached for his hammer as the weapon grazed his shoulder.

He sprang into Crowell's chest to counter the blade. The cut on his shoulder must have sliced deeper than he thought as he rammed into him. It burned with a pain that caused him to grit his teeth and jump back toward the forge.

Crowell shook his head and threw the dagger at Sindrick's throat.

Sindrick tried to block it, catching the point in his forearm above his bracers. He cried out in pain and swung at Crowell, who rushed to attack. Before it connected with his head, Crowell's massive hands caught the hammer and ripped it from Sindrick's grasp.

Sindrick froze, mesmerized at the unnatural ability Crowell controlled. No one should have been able to stop such a blow.

His thoughts were shattered by a boot that slammed into his hip. It twisted him to the ground, falling prone with his back to Crowell.

"Stop this," Sindrick pleaded. He rolled away in time to watch the hammer splinter the board he had landed on. "Please, it was an accident."

"You murdered her in cold blood." Crowell dropped the tool and held up his fists. "She held a power greater than all of us and wanted to share it with me."

"She was my wife!" Sindrick shook with anger.

Instead of waiting for Crowell to respond, Sindrick lunged at him. He connected a solid blow to Crowell's jaw, but the man hardly moved.

The wind burst out from Sindrick's mouth as Crowell's fist punched his stomach.

The room grew hazy, and he felt himself falling to the ground again. Pain coursed through his body.

"You are a murderer! Murderer!" Crowell repeated to himself. "Eleanor was greater than you could imagine. She wanted to leave. You wouldn't allow it. You did this."

Sindrick lifted his head to see Crowell pacing and muttering curses behind him.

He snatched Sindrick's feet and pulled him away from the forge. Sindrick tried to kick free, but his attacks no longer phased Crowell, who kept chanting to himself.

"You are not a killer!" Sindrick shouted, trying to break whatever spell had possessed Crowell. "You won't kill your friend."

Crowell stopped dragging Sindrick and looked at the ceiling.

"No," he said and grabbed a ruby shard of the broken scabbard. The intent to kill sang from within it. "I would have killed Gostav if he was this close. He was a murderer. You are the murderer—Gostav."

His eyes turned utterly black. He cried out in the strange language he had spoken on the ship.

Sindrick secured his bracers and reached into his pocket for the fire stones.

Crowell stretched his hand out toward him, but Sindrick slammed the rocks onto the ground, causing them to erupt with fire. It reacted against the dark magic in the air and furiously circled them.

Crowell stumbled to the open door while the flames continued to swirl around the room. They filled the place with a cloud of dense smoke. Sindrick coughed as the heat intensified.

The fire licked across the ceiling, causing the support beams to pop and snap from its destructive force. Even through his armor, Sindrick's skin started to blister and scorch.

He tried to flee when the crushing grip of Crowell's new strength yanked him across the floor.

"You won't get away," Crowell snarled and stood in the doorway. "I'll kill you, murderer."

Crowell lifted the shard above his head. Time seemed to stop, Sindrick heard the screams of those witnessing the event from outside, and the roar of something else.

It moved like a blur, but caught part of Crowell's face, ripping him outside the building.

"Go back to the hills!" Crowell yelled. "I'll finish you for good!"

Sindrick propped himself up to see what saved him. The horrific beast towered over Crowell, who struck it repeatedly. Its white fur seemed thicker than iron and produced a frosty mist around it.

Crowell managed to jab his thumbs into the creature's bulbous eyes. It reared back in pain, exposing rows of teeth with a mouth that could swallow an average man whole.

A sharp crack above Sindrick pierced the commotion in front of him. Blazing planks and stone fell across the threshold of the door. There was no escape.

"This way!" a familiar voice called out near the back of the shop.

Sindrick crawled toward the sound. Malek beckoned for him to hurry through a small window.

With his last remaining energy, Sindrick escaped into the open air. He scrambled away from the burning building with his former master, watching their years of work turn to ash.

21

A crowd formed around Crowell and the beast. They would have seen Sindrick engulfed by flames in the forge, assuming he perished. Without the bracers, he would not have survived the horrific fire, and no one but Malek knew what they could do. Crowell would not look for him anymore. The fearsome captain would say he avenged Eleanor's death and sail away.

"No one else can have you," her voice whispered with the wind.

Sindrick shuddered at the strange presence lingering in his thoughts. She watched him from beyond the realm of reality.

"Leave me alone," he muttered to himself and gripped his brittle hair.

Large chunks of it came out, leaving him nearly bald due to the intense heat he endured.

He looked toward the north. The journey no one returned from in the frozen hills was his only option. Yet, no one had the bracers he wore to protect them from the elements.

"I saw the same look in your father's eyes," Malek said beside Sindrick and coughed. "The shop is gone now. Perhaps I should —"

His voice was drowned out by a terrible scream coming from the crowd.

Sindrick rushed around the building to see the summoned creature backing away from Crowell. The fierce captain held up a small child between him and the beast. Behind them was a growing crowd of villagers.

"No!" Rena screamed again. "Put him down."

"What are you doing?" Sindrick yelled at Crowell.

"Stay back!" he commanded. "You shouldn't be alive."

"Please, give the child to his mother," Sindrick pleaded. "Take me instead. It's me you want to kill."

"No." Crowell glared at him through one eye. The other was missing, and his face had a large gash across it from the beast. "Come any closer, and I'll take the boy's life."

217

"Why are you doing this?" Dan cried out. "Give me back my son!"

Dan tried to get closer, but the summoned beast lashed out at him. Some of the other villagers jabbed at it with their weapons. It started to slink toward Crowell.

"Don't you see what's happening?" Sindrick said, continuing to approach him. "Your corrupted magic has made you worse than those you hate."

Crowell glanced at the beast and then back to Sindrick. He snarled with a defeated look in his eye. Gripping the child tighter, he fled in the direction of the docks.

The others were unable to follow as the beast kept them pinned. Sindrick sprinted after Crowell. His lungs burned as he tried to catch up, but the captain moved with incredible speed. By the time he reached the docks, the ship was already loose on the water.

"Come back!" Sindrick yelled. "Take me, not the boy!"

His words fell unanswered while the vessel disappeared into the fog of night.

"Where is he?" Dan called out, running up to Sindrick. "Where is Crowell? What happened to my son?"

Sindrick opened his mouth to speak, but he couldn't find the right words to say. He hung his head and stared into the empty space where the Stormeye once rested.

"I'm sorry," he said softly.

Dan fell to his knees and wept.

"Something took over Crowell," Sindrick said and sat next to his friend. "I couldn't get to him in time."

A small group approached the two with Rena at the center. She held her stomach and burst into tears.

"Aldrnari is a strong boy." Dan stood and embraced his wife. "There is nothing we can do now but pray he will find his way back to us."

"I'll find Crowell and get him back for you." Sindrick got up quickly and winced from the pain of his burns.

"No, you've done enough." Dan placed his hand on Sindrick's shoulder. "Trying to find that madman would only drive you down the same path. We must rebuild what was lost."

Sindrick wanted to say more but knew his friend was right. His steps had already led him to the cliff of madness, and he had gazed into its endless abyss. The tragedy of Eleanor had been caused by her own dark deeds and Crowell's ambition. Or perhaps it was the amulet. Whatever the case, he could not blame himself any longer.

"I wanted to tell you sooner," Malek said, stepping out of the crowd. "My time to retire from the forge is imminent. I will help you make a new one for Virfell and leave you to master it. You are ready to take on your own apprentices."

"Thank you," Sindrick said. He turned toward the smoking rubble in the distance. "What about the creature?"

"It's gone," Rena said between sobs. "Jack gave it a killing blow. The others tore it apart."

"We can talk about it more in the morning," Dan said and held Rena's hand. "Let's go home. This night has been hard enough."

Sindrick followed them back into town. He helped clean some of the creature's remains off the streets and wandered into the tavern. The realization that he wouldn't have a place to stay made him long for a drink. Sleep would be scarce for a while.

Sindrick finished moving the final anvil in place at his new workshop. The entire town had helped him construct the building and provided many supplies. At last, he could sit down and rest in the new Virfell forge.

His finger rubbed across one of the materials in his bag, and it pricked his skin. He pulled it out, holding it close to the light from the flames.

"You haven't left me," Sindrick said as he recognized the wooden material. "I suppose you will remain a secret until age takes your memory away."

He pressed the wood to his lips.

"How did I fall for your lies?" he asked himself as a solitary tear ran down his cheek.

"You believe you had a choice in any of this?" her voice responded with the shadows, dancing around the back of the wall. "Your heart is murderous."

"Go away!" he shouted and threw the wood at the forge.

The shard bounced and rolled into the fire. Sindrick watched it turn red, but it did not ignite. No matter what he would do, he could not destroy it.

It would remain with him, haunting his memories. The memory of the one he loved and lost. The one whose name was etched onto the title of a ship, floating alone and abandoned in a hidden cave.

Matthew E. Nordin

The Salty Eleanor.

EPILOGUE

"How long have you been sailing with him?" the young cabin boy asked, securing the rigging against the growing waves.

"A fair amount of time," the woman said and raised her spyglass to gaze at the approaching storm. "Well before he last set foot on land. I was there when it happened, and he vowed to stay at sea."

"The cook said he hasn't left our ship for at least seven years." The boy stared across the waters with a concerned look. "Are you sure we should sail through that?"

"That's nothing," she said and slapped him on the back. "I watched him fight a beast with his bare hands and rip off the massive tentacles of a leviathan." She wriggled her arms around

223

and laughed. "We have nothing to fear but crossing him. Make haste and get under. He'll be out shortly."

No sooner had she spoken than the door to the captain's cabin swung open. A large and intimidating man stepped onto the deck. The crew barely reached his shoulders in height. His legs looked thicker than the mast, and a frightful scar covered half of his face.

"Keep her steady," the captain called out, flashing a jagged row of teeth. "We need to punch through the gale before nightfall."

"Are we going to hunt the trolls again?" the boy whispered to the woman.

She nodded and walked up to the captain. "The ship's ready for you."

"Thank you, Brittany," the captain said and waved her off. He pointed to the boy. "You there, come for a walk."

The boy rushed to his side. "What do you need me to do, sir?"

"I noticed you copying my maps when you thought I was asleep." The captain made his way across the deck with the boy close behind. "Show them to me."

The boy reluctantly reached down and pulled a rolled-up paper out of his pant leg. Before he could explain himself, the captain snatched it from him.

"Those red dots you have here," the captain said, pointing at the spots on the poorly drawn map. "They are the private locations where the troll island was reported to float. How did you place them?"

"I know you told me not to read your journal, but I like the stories of your hunts." The boy looked at his feet. "I figured out where the creatures might be coming from and wanted to help you find them."

"You have a hidden talent. Don't stop your search."

"Can I ask you something?" the boy said quietly. "What is this area at the top? You don't have any words for it on your map, and there are lots of lines crossing it off."

"I'm sure you've heard the stories of the northern lands and. . . Virfell." The captain clenched his fists. "That's where I saved you from a terrible attack. The beast is still there, waiting for me to return."

"Sometimes, I hear Brittany talking about it." The boy nodded toward her. "She said it was always cold. Are we going there?"

"No, lad. It is a vile place." The captain glared at him. "You mustn't think of it, ever."

"I'm sorry. I will keep it marked off my map too."

The captain's composure softened. "That you should. Tell me, if you were to look for the troll king, where do you think he would be?"

"I think he's here, by the big green area." The boy perked up and put his finger on his drawing. "The red marks move in that direction all the time."

"The forest of the fae? Interesting." The captain looked across the open sea. "It would make sense for them. The trolls are known for their ability to counter the fae's magic. Perhaps they like to be close to their enemy."

"Does this mean we're going to Northeal? You write about it a lot."

"You are not to leave the ship." The captain leaned down and held out his palm. "Your wandering fingers would get you into too much trouble in a village like that."

The boy glanced back and forth. He reached into his vest and pulled out Brittany's spyglass.

"I wanted to see the storm like she did," he said.

"In other places, there'd be a severe reprimand for your misdeeds." The captain took the piece and held it up for the woman to see. "I might find a good use for those skills when you're older. For now, keep to the ship and stay in my cabin. Do not leave until I say. I'll have someone fetch your meals."

"Thank you, sir," the boy said, knowing the captain was done with his company.

Brittany glared at him while he rushed to the cabin door.

"Are you sure it's wise to leave him alone in your room?" he overheard her say to the captain.

"He knows not to steal from me." The captain shot the boy a stern look. "I see everything."

"The storm's moving up fast," Brittany said. "We should be in the thick of it soon."

"They don't call my ship the Stormeye for nothing," the captain said and grinned. "If we carry on through the night, we can reach Northeal's waters in the morning. I'll stay with the boy when we reach the harbor. I need to ask him more about his map."

"Do you suspect our little Aldrnari can find him? No one's heard from the troll king since your last encounter."

"I won't let anyone slip by me again, especially Gostav. The seas belong to me now." The captain braced himself at the wheel and stared into the storm. "I'll destroy the other one too, if I ever come across that blacksmith again." His eye became dark like the harsh clouds approaching. "Crowell is on the hunt."

ACKNOWLEDGMENTS

My thanks begin with the "Father of lights, with whom can be no variation, nor turning shadow" (James 1:17 WEB)

I also have to thank the purest heart I know, my beautiful wife, Lisa. Her editing insight makes my creative process more delightful.

Many thanks to the beta readers on this work: Crystal, Megan, Jennifer, & Joe. There was so much you helped me create in this story.

Thank you to my friends and family, who are always supporting my writing (sorry if this one got too dark again, mom).

And last, but certainly not the least, an overwhelming thank you to all who read this book. If I could hug each one of you for spending time in my stories, I would!

From the bottom of my caffeine-ridden heart,
Thank you!

If you've enjoyed this story, please consider leaving a review and find all of Matthew's books on Amazon:

SHADOWS OF ELEANOR

HOLLOWS OF THE NOX

A young scholar discovers a book of ancient sorcery. It challenges his understanding of magic and beacons him to embark upon a journey to find the source of its power.

AWAKENING THE STRICKEN

At the fringes of the elven kingdom, a young sorceress works on perfecting her mother's spells. Yet an evil force may be stronger than her desire to court one of the guards.

THE SALTY ELEANOR

An alchemist born to a blacksmith finds his passion in the earth's elements. Everything changes when he meets someone more enchanting than his weapons.

THE PYCROFT UNIVERSE

THE PYCROFT PARTICLE

Doctor Patricia Pycroft is set to revolutionize the travel industry with the discovery of teleportation. When strange occurrences happen, her work and faith are questioned.

PYCROFT CONTINUUM

(coming soon)

MUSINGS OF THE NORTHERN POET:

POEMS OF LOVE AND FAITH

ABOUT THE AUTHOR

Matthew E. Nordin is a speculative fiction writer and a Midwestern traveler. He is secretly formulating a series of fantasy novels with a dash of science fiction tales to spice things up. His love of renaissance faires, conventions, and writing workshops have spurred his passion for setting his thoughts into print.

He met his wife while performing with the newly renamed group: Scenery Changes. Together, they specialize in improv comedy shows & acting workshops; creating artistic works & writing; living a simple life & most of all, having fun!

Join in their adventures at
www.scenerychanges.com

Stage & Scene & In-Between

Made in the USA
Middletown, DE
07 June 2021

40993758R00142